EVIL RIVER

EVIL RIVER

KEITH JACOBSEN

The Book Guild Ltd

First published in Great Britain in 2020 by
The Book Guild Ltd
9 Priory Business Park
Wistow Road, Kibworth
Leicestershire, LE8 0RX
Freephone: 0800 999 2982
www.bookguild.co.uk
Email: info@bookguild.co.uk
Twitter: @bookguild

Typeset in 12pt Adobe Jenson Pro

Printed and bound in the UK by TJ International, Padstow, Cornwall

ISBN 978 1913208 301

British Library Cataloguing in Publication Data.
A catalogue record for this book is available from the British Library.

FOREWORD

I never met Alan Harris, the author of the pages which
follow. I knew him only by his reputation as one of the
foremost scholars in his field. That field being also mine,
though I could claim no distinction to match his or come
anywhere near, I sought his help in the course of an extensive
correspondence after his retirement. His responses were
so thorough and the guidance he offered so generous that
the career which I have since followed, which has been not
without its modest successes, owes more to him than I could
ever have repaid.

Alan died as many of us would wish, no prior symptoms
to alert him, found without breath on a summer afternoon,
seated in his garden, surrounded by his beloved rose bushes,
a smile on his face. A tranquil end to a life lived the same
way, one may be forgiven for thinking, and, to judge from
his obituaries, so thought most of his former colleagues and
students. He was by all accounts a bachelor don typical of an
era long gone. He lived within the confines of his college and

the inner boundaries of his discipline, untroubled by the wider world beyond, its dangers and its passions unknown to him. I was ready to believe that. Until I made my chance discovery.

His death came as a surprise and a shock to me. In his letters he had always assured me of his continuing robust health. The researches for which I had sought his help and hoped for much more were still incomplete. I was therefore relieved when upon enquiring of the Master of his former college I was told that Alan had left his entire stock of books and papers to the college, where they could be consulted at any time of my choosing in the beautiful old library. I took an overdue sabbatical from my duties at Harvard and went to Europe, setting aside several weeks of the summer term to spend in Oxford in the company of Alan's legacy. I had been warned that the papers were still in boxes and were not sorted. He had filed them in an apparently random fashion, no doubt expecting that he would have time to put them in order.

I soon found what I needed for my research. It was on my last day there, when I was refiling the papers in what I hoped would be a more orderly system to aid future scholars, that I found this account, neatly typed in a buff folder, placed among an assortment of ephemera, most of them to do with local parish or gardening club activities in which he was engaged. My first thoughts were that he had belatedly turned his hand to the writing of fiction and had decided that the result did not merit any more prominent place within his own papers, never mind the wider world. But a taste for fiction, even as an afterthought, seemed out of character, or at least out of the impression of his character I had formed up to then. I took the folder back to my hotel and read it in a single sitting, becoming ever more convinced as I read that it was all true, compiled with the honesty and thoroughness for which he was known in his work. Without permission, telling myself that in so doing I was in no way detracting from the contribution to scholarship which his legacy to the college intended, I took the folder with me back to the States. I read and reread it many times. It was not only that I was haunted by the events he describes. My own eyes had been opened, painfully. I was humbled to find that my assumptions about Alan Harris, while not wholly false, were only part of the truth and a very small and insignificant part at that. What price now the impressions and judgements I so readily made about everybody I met, including those I thought I knew well? Here in these pages is no ivory tower scholar cut off from the world, though that description would have justly fitted his whole adult life but for a single tragic event which drove him against all instinct and habit to leave the shelter of the walls he had built to protect himself and seek out a much more important truth than any to be found in academia. He faced danger. He forced himself to look into his own soul and to reopen deep wounds he had long since consigned to the oblivion which conceals but never heals. And afterwards? He told nobody. He returned to his former life as if nothing had happened. Nobody outside the few who already knew suspected a thing. Perhaps the smile on his face as he died meant that he had come to terms with the regrets and lost opportunities he here records. I would like to think so. Or maybe it was just a chance disposition of his facial muscles at the moment his heart stopped. Academics like me should know better than to jump to conclusions which cannot be verified.

In that same spirit, and despite my conviction from the start as to the truth of what I had read, I decided to see if I could find witnesses to that truth. I found two. Dr Alban Knight is now a distinguished scholar in his own right, at Berkeley. I visited him there and we read through it together. By the end, he was crying. He could only nod when I asked him if it was all true to his knowledge. I then returned to England, where I at last managed to track down someone from a very different walk of life but who played just as important a role, Major Max, as he is herein called. He too verified the account, though in his case he maintained the military bearing with which he is credited throughout and shed no tears, though I sensed that he might do so once I had left.

Both agreed that while Alan had clearly never intended publication, neither had he proscribed it. He had not destroyed the contents of the folder. He had left its discovery to fate, and fate for some obscure reason had chosen me. Neither Alban nor Max had any objection to publication. But what of the boy to whom Alan's account is addressed, to whom he makes so many intimate confessions he would never have made in real life? I will speak for him, Alban told me, and I know he is content.

So I leave you in Alan's hands.

Dr James Fraser
Harvard
2003

ONE

By Oak Walk in the University Parks the Cherwell divides. A tributary, heavy with drifting sediment and rotting logs and overshadowed by precariously rooted oaks and willows, wanders sluggishly eastward and then south through a patchwork of muddy fields and water meadows with names such as Bat Willow, Music, and Angel and Greyhound, before rejoining the main course of the river on the far side of Magdalen Bridge and Christchurch Meadow. Along the tributary, just beyond the fork and before a bend, streams and rivulets feed a stagnant bulge. Heavy and prolonged spring rains such as we had that year do not make the flow any faster here. Water overflowing the banks seeps into the meadow mud, creating tiny pools and lakes trapped into stillness below but abuzz on the surface with the whirl and whirr of a carnival of biting insects. One of the feeder streams is Peasmoor Brook, rising a mile away in Marston village. Where the brook empties into the placid water of the bulge is where they found your punt. Empty.

Further downstream the tributary is bisected by a stretch of narrow island called Mesopotamia Walk. A single-file path leads the casual walker between clusters of celandine clinging to the eastern bank and lines of white and crack willow planted to hold firm the lower-lying western one. No doubt some witty don (an idle bachelor like myself?) had conferred the exotic name on the otherwise unremarkable stretch of island, noticing it lay, if not between two rivers exactly, then at least between two watercourses. What he may not have known is that the eastern course had once been a millstream. At the southern end it narrows to no more than a few feet, funnelled between stone walls. Where the mill once plied its laborious trade a double wooden sluice gate is all that remains, pressed down by iron ratchet levers. When there is the threat of flood the levers are used to raise the gates, turning the stone below into a weir over which the corralled waters cascade angrily.

It was in such a flood time that they found you, carried there by the undertow created by the raising of the sluice, trapped against the gate, grotesquely swollen, wrapped in a shroud of leaves and branches.

TWO

'What is your full name, please, sir?'
The inspector's manner was bored, detached.
So a drunken, over-privileged student had fallen in the river and drowned. So what? Good riddance if you ask me. One less burden on the taxpayer. Just my bloody luck to have a job in a place full of them. He did not say any of those things. He did not have to. He was in late middle age, probably nearing retirement. He wore a drab overcoat for all seasons over a crumpled brown suit. A stained yellow tie hung loose over a check shirt. He sat in one of the armchairs normally occupied by my students in tutorials, something which caused a feeling of resentment to well up in me. The last time I saw you, you were sitting in that same chair, reading your weekly essay. The sergeant stood by the inspector's shoulder, youthful, upright, attentive and smartly dressed, taking notes with crisp enthusiasm, getting ready for the day when he would take his colleague's place. I had the impression that for both of them that day could not come soon enough.

I wondered what they would think of the room. In their presence I was embarrassed by its size, the port-stained splendour of the huge oak desk, the narrow gothic windows, the portraits of unknown scholars from past generations, the books lining the walls and spilling onto the floor, the ornate cupboard where I kept the sherry to be brought out only on special occasions. But, apart from the sherry and my own modest contribution to the stock of books, I had had nothing to do with the room. I had inherited it complete with the unclaimed contents from the previous occupant, a history don, another bachelor. I had changed nothing. On the basis of a single article he had written on post-war industrial relations which had gained widespread attention on both sides of the Atlantic, he had received an offer from an Ivy League college and left at indecently short notice. My own subject area was far more narrow and blessedly irrelevant to the modern world of which I knew and understood so little. I knew a similar offer would never come my way. I also knew that if by some miracle one did, I would not have the courage to accept it.

'My name is Harris. Alan Harris.'

'Dr Harris?'

'No. Plain mister.'

'And where do you live, sir?'

'Here. There is a small living space through there.' I pointed to a door in the far corner of the room. 'I am what is known as a bachelor don. A relic of the past. A curio. There used to be lots of us. Now we are a dying breed.'

A small space indeed, also inherited and unchanged, but it suited me well enough. Beyond the door was a narrow, cell-like bedroom with a hard single bed and one high lattice window. The shower, toilet and sink were crammed into a corner behind a curtain. A cupboard contained tea, coffee and biscuits, with room for very little else. As in a cheap hotel, an electric kettle, cups, saucers and plates, two of each, stood on the uncluttered surface. I would have been ashamed of the utilitarian nature of my living space except that nobody ever saw it, only the scout when he came in to clean and make up the bed. No need for anyone to feel shame before a scout. They have seen it all and know far more than they ever let on.

The inspector frowned, wondering perhaps if I were having some sort of obscure academic joke at his expense.

'And how old are you, sir?'

'Forty-six.'

'You were his tutor?'

'Yes. His college tutor. He did Anglo-Saxon literature with me. He went outside for other subjects.'

'Outside?'

'To tutors in other colleges. Experts in their fields. It's the same for everybody.'

'According to the Master his full name was Simon James Harvey.'

'Yes. I mean, if the Master says so. I never knew his middle name.'

'When did you last see him?'

'At his last tutorial. Week before last.'

'Where?'

'Here. In this room. As usual. He sat where you are.'

The inspector shuffled uncomfortably. There might have been a slightly sharp tone to my last remark. The sergeant smiled and took another note.

'Anybody else present?'

'No. Just the two of us. He was the only one in his year doing my period.'

'How did he seem?'

'Seem?'

'Anything unusual. Did he seem anxious, depressed?'

I felt a sudden wave of nausea.

'Depressed? Inspector, are you suggesting he might have taken his own life?'

It happens. Far too often. Every year. Almost all of them unexpected, impossible to anticipate. It is what every senior college member dreads. A suicide among the flock for whom we have a duty of care. A reminder that the radiant young people filling the air around us with youth and confidence are still barely out of childhood. They deserve space and freedom. God knows they have earned it. At the same time they need to be watched. As I did not watch you.

'Just enquiring, sir. Not ruling anything out. Not at this stage.'

His expression was impassive, professional.

'But I thought it was an accident. I heard…'

'Yes, sir. What did you hear?'

'He fell out of a punt and drowned.'

The inspector paused and coughed, appearing to be asking himself how far he should go in sharing with me.

'We think he was in a punt that day, yes. But you don't just fall out of a punt, do you? Not to drown, that is. I wouldn't know, myself, of course. But young Pearson over here tells me he was a student in this place.' He nodded towards the sergeant who smiled again and took yet another note. 'Oxford, I mean. Bright young spark is Pearson. Got his eye on my job and as far as I'm concerned he can have it tomorrow. Anyway, he was telling me about it on the way down here. It seems you can fall in if the pole gets stuck in the mud. But the river only comes up to your waist. Sobers you up if you've had one too many up at the Vicky. That's what Pearson tells me it's called. The Victoria Arms. By the river, up at Marston. Where you go by punt on a summer evening. Then on the way back you've lost all inhibitions.

Get too confident with the pole in those sticky bits and you can find that you with pole attached and the punt have parted company. Happens a lot, so Pearson tells me. It's a bit demeaning but you don't drown. You know about punting yourself, I suppose. As an Oxford man.'

I don't. Not personally. I know it is what the undergraduates do in summer. A perfect way to spend a languorous afternoon on the river. I like to watch them from the bank. The easy, slurpy glide of the boat through the still water, the casual chatter and laughter, all thoughts of the essay deadline or looming examination banished for a few hours. Only I have never been punting, actively or passively. I was a student here myself, in the same college where I now teach. I knew three glorious undergraduate summers, an experience like no other. But somehow I was always too busy for punting. Or was it that nobody invited me and I was too shy to make an invitation myself, too self-conscious to make a fool of myself by taking that forbiddingly long pole into my hands, afraid I should immediately fall in and become an object of ridicule? The message then ringing in my ears was the same as in all the years that came before and after. Do not try it, whatever it might be. Do not take a risk. Be safe.

I was suddenly angry, an emotion so unusual for me that at first I failed to recognise it.

'You're suggesting he had been drinking far too much, Inspector? A lot more than one too many? Went up to the Victoria Arms, drank to excess even by student standards, lost control of the pole on the way back and fell in? I suppose, what with the effects of the drink and the shock of the water he couldn't climb back into the punt or up the bank so he…'

I was searching desperately for an explanation. An accident, I heard myself telling the distraught parents. A terrible, bizarre accident. I am so sorry for your loss. But not a suicide. Not that. Please God, not a suicide. Not one of mine.

'If I might say so, sir, it is you rather than I who seem to be making most of the suggestions here.'

'I'm sorry, Inspector. There are a lot of stories doing the rounds. And with no hard information...'

'I understand, sir. But you haven't answered my question. Did he seem unduly anxious or depressed?'

'No. The opposite. He was beginning to blossom. It happens sometimes that way, with the quiet ones. They come out of their shell in the end, but it can take a long time. His work was improving. He seemed relaxed, happy, even. He smiled more than he ever had done, made the odd jocose remark. Not much chance of that with my subject, usually, but sometimes he would see a humorous aspect to something which had eluded me.'

'He was like that at the last tutorial, week before last?' The sergeant was scribbling. 'He was... how did you put it? Oh yes. Jocose?'

He pronounced it not with the accent on the second syllable, as I had, but like "cocoa". He was making a point. Only a supercilious academic like me would have chosen that word. I had given him something to throw back at me, a means to discomfort me, and already he was smiling through the sarcasm. Why hadn't I just said "funny"?

'He seemed in a good mood, Inspector. He read me the essay I had set him. It was good. Not excellent. He was never going to be that. He was never material for a first. But it was good work. A real improvement on last term. Beta plus.'

'Sorry?'

There was an unmistakeable sneer on his face now. I had handed him another missile.

'Our marking system. A very good essay gets an alpha. A really excellent one an alpha plus. Beta is good. So beta plus is more than just good but not... not quite alpha. It's sort of in between.'

It always sounds precious whenever I try to explain it like that to an outsider, and the expression on his face did not disguise his contempt.

'Really, sir? Don't know why you don't just mark them out of ten, like they did at our school. No doubt Pearson can explain the finer points to me later. So, he didn't seem to you to be distracted in any way?'

'No. There was nothing unusual about the tutorial. He paid attention to my comments. Made notes. Asked sensible questions. I set him another essay. For last week. For the tutorial he never turned up for.'

'And did he make a note of the assignment?'

'Oh, yes. He was always very conscientious about that. He did his research carefully. Planned his essays well. Only he had just begun to show much more imagination and a livelier style. I would say he was well on track for a good second. When he first arrived I was beginning to wonder if he would only manage a third.'

He managed to frown and sneer at the same time. 'Second or third what, sir? Attempt?'

For God's sake, surely he understood what I was talking about? Was he keeping his boredom at bay by deliberately trying to rile me? If so, it was my fault. I had again fallen into the trap of using university jargon.

'No, Inspector. I was referring to our system for classifying degrees. What the students get when they leave, after doing their final examinations. There are three main classes. The very best get a first. Most get seconds or thirds. Some get a fourth, or a pass.' I was in deep water now but irritation drove me on.

'They say a fourth is the hardest to get. Quite an achievement. You have to pitch it just right. A few marks either side and it's a third or a pass. And a pass is perilously close to a fail. No doubt Pearson can explain to you. Later.'

He smiled, as if to concede at least a draw. He turned to Pearson, took his notebook from him and read what he had entered, muttering and nodding to himself. Pearson looked around the room, perhaps indulging in a rare opportunity for nostalgia for his own student days. For the time being they had forgotten my presence. Then the inspector looked up again.

'What about his outside activities? His interests? Friends, girlfriends?'

'He was involved in music in the college. I can say that. But there's not much more I can say. Nothing about his personal life. The undergraduates get on with their own lives.'

'What did he play? Electric guitar?'

'No, the piano was his instrument. Classical. Chamber groups. That sort of thing.'

The inspector's sneer this time was both visible and audible. 'Did he drink? Or take drugs? Or both?'

'Most of the students drink. But not to excess. That is my impression, despite what you seem to think. Well, maybe some do. But Simon never seemed to me to be an excess sort of person.'

'And drugs?' he asked.

'I can't imagine that was his scene.'

'But you said he was coming out of his shell.'

'Yes, but not in that way. Not in a rebellious way. Not pushing against social norms like that, taking risks with his own body, just to make a point, the way some do. I just can't imagine he would have done that. He might have found some new friends. Someone special, maybe. Or just become more comfortable with himself. How awful for something like this to happen, just when...'

'Yes, sir?'

'I was going to say, just when life was starting to open up for him.'

THREE

A s life had never opened up for me. But that was my choice. I had devoted my life to finding walls and hiding behind them.

So my college and I are well suited to each other. How would I describe it to an outsider? The north-facing outer walls are strung out along St Giles', three stories of warm sandstone with narrow leaded windows beneath pointed arches, a squat gate tower sitting above the massive main entrance. The aspect is forbidding and welcoming at the same time, beckoning me to the refuge within while repelling any who do not belong. Inside are more walls surrounding the quads. Beyond them, through the round arches of an Italianate colonnade, paths lead around and through a wide sweep of lawn lovingly tended to a state of close-knit perfection over many decades. Beyond the lawn, shrubs, beeches and a rockery offer seclusion and inviting shade. The college garden is justly famous. It is a walled garden, of course.

For years I sheltered within those walls, believing myself

to be safe, until the day when something, someone, tore them down, left me open and defenceless against the storms of the vast, terrifying world beyond. That someone was you, Simon.

When did we first meet? Two years ago, when you came up from school to be interviewed. It was the final test which would confirm your admission to the college and the university, your chance to pull yourself across the finishing line, mine to reassure myself and the tutor on admissions that you were worthy of the privilege. You were sitting in that same chair which the inspector had usurped. I was trying desperately to draw you out. You were painfully shy. But I knew already that I liked you, that you would be a rewarding student to teach. Far more rewarding than those who exude self-confidence from the moment they first walk through the door, who would never admit or even see their own shortcomings, who would do well enough in the end but would always lack the insight and capacity for self-criticism without which they would never add any depth or originality to what had been spoon-fed to them at school. I was desperate for you to give me just enough so I could recommend acceptance. You had very good A levels. But that was never enough. There had to be more. A reason to take you when so many others with A levels just as good had to be turned down. You seemed at last to sense what I needed. You stammered it out. You were musical, sort of, you told me. After a fashion. Not brilliant, but it was very important to you. You were running a music appreciation society in your sixth form. You would hope to do something similar at college, if you were fortunate enough to be admitted. It was enough. I smiled, trying to send you that wordless message, that you had said enough and need torture yourself no more. I would recommend acceptance. I stood up and you did the same in the same instant. We shook hands, remember? I could not

13

tell you there and then that you were in. I did not have the final say. But I knew my recommendation would secure your entry. The tutor on admissions trusted my judgement and I had never let him down in the past. I longed to tell you of my decision, but that was strictly forbidden. You would have to go home and wait for the formal letter.

That same evening after my interview with the inspector, I sat alone in my room. No, not alone. You were there, in your usual chair. You could not tell me any more about yourself than you had already, which was little enough, and far too little to explain what happened on the river that day. But I could tell you about me. You had not asked. That was not your place. It had been my role to open out to you so you could open out to me. I had failed. I had kept too great a distance between us, another wall in fact. Now, when it was too late, I could start to break it down. As the shadows crept across the room, your form, tall, slender, leaning slightly forward as always, took shape in the chair, your expression of nervous curiosity and wonder clearly visible.

What shall I tell you first? How did I come to be here? Would you be interested to know about that?

This place is a long way in time and spirit from my early childhood in a Liverpool suburb, though in those days walls defined my life as much as they do now. Those of my cramped and dingy primary school kept the outside world at bay but enclosed me within a dangerous space from which there was no escape.

Not so much the classroom as the playground. There, for some reason, we were left unsupervised. It was no more than a tarmacked space, useful only for movement (no ball games allowed), alone or in gangs. I never knew if the gang who targeted me had a name. I doubt it. They did not need one. They had their own use for the prison-high wall which bounded one side of the playground. They would pin me against it and punch me in the stomach, solemnly, methodically, joylessly, each taking it in turns. I never knew why, unless it was because I had joined the school after the start of the year, the result of a minor bout of measles, after all the gangs had been formed and their hierarchies established. Too late to insinuate myself into one of them. What did I have to offer? I was pale and weak and, worst of all, studious. I wore glasses. These needed replacing several times, until I learned to leave them in my desk before slipping into the playground, hoping with a perverse childish logic that if I could not see my tormentors they would not be able to see me. The glasses were a favourite target, for those bored with stomach punching. They could be pulled off and stamped on, while my hands were occupied in trying to defend other parts. There were others like me in the gangs, but unlike me they had something to offer. Generous pocket money enabled them to buy their way in and secure ongoing protection.

I had already started to build my own walls, the ones nobody could see. I could hide behind them, even while I was being hit. I have them to this day. In those days they took the form of lists, numbers, vocabularies, formulae, anything I could pick up in lessons or in reading at home and commit to silent memory. They earned me the label of swot, which only served to make my punishments in the playground all the more relentless.

So was this how I ended up an expert on Anglo-Saxon language and literature, the choice which would mean that in due course our paths would inevitably cross? The subject has its own walls. It is not a fluid, constantly shifting area of study like physics or chemistry. The language does not live and change as the world around changes. There is a fixed corpus of source work to which, by definition, nothing has been added for centuries. It is not entirely safe, of course. New discoveries are occasionally made by scholars with far more energy and curiosity than I will ever have, manuscripts brought to light in dusty libraries, artefacts unearthed by archaeologists which explain a date or a reference or undermine some long-cherished theory. But revelations such as these are rare and do not shake the foundations of my own modest researches. I can absorb them comfortably, with no sense of threat.

FOUR

Your absence was not thought anything remarkable at first, though it was not like you to fail to turn up for a tutorial, not without letting me know.

I put it down to a sudden cold or an attack of flu. I waited for the note of apology and explanation, or the knock on the door. None came. I enquired of some of your fellow students when I saw them in the quad. It had been days since they had seen you. I asked your staircase scout. He told me your bed had not been slept in for those same days. That had to mean you had gone away for personal reasons. A funeral, or a sudden family illness, perhaps. But you would need an exeat. I asked the bursar. You had not applied for one.

A sombre atmosphere soon descended on the whole college. It was uncanny how a sudden mood of disquiet could so quickly spread through an institution known for a cheerfulness at times bordering on brashness. Within twenty-four hours the new mood had permeated the sandstone walls of the exterior and the quads and the stained-glass windows of the chapel, lent its unmistakeable hue to the whispers and murmurs in the library, subdued the normally noisy clatter of dinner in hall. My anxious enquiries had been passed on and were multiplying, now leavened with rumours of varying degrees of plausibility as to the cause of your absence. Soon there would be talk of little else. In the Senior Common Room word quickly got around that the police had been discreetly informed, and your parents alerted.

Then the news broke, confirming suspicions which had been gathering an aura of certainty for several days. You were dead. Your body had been found on the river.

A few days after the inspector and Sergeant Pearson had interviewed me, the Master sent me a note asking me to call on him for sherry at his lodgings.

The title of Master of an Oxford college is something of a misnomer. There was nothing remotely masterly about the nature of the post or the manner of its present incumbent. A Master is only *primus inter pares*, he liked to say. A committee man, an administrator, a coordinator, a mediator, a persuader, a beggar for funds, a shoulder to cry on. He is all these things as well as he can be, but the one thing he is not is a dictator.

Dr Groves would not have known how to be a dictator, even if he had suddenly found himself placed in that position at the head of an army coup in Latin America or the Middle East. He was a historian of minor distinction who had to his credit only one publication, a slim study of the role of the state in relation to the citizen down the centuries. It was not easy to get hold of a copy, though the college library always kept one strictly for reference only. Not that anyone had referred to it for years, judging from the layer of dust clinging to it when I decided one day to consult it with a view to adding to the small stock of subjects on which he and I could have a conversation. It is a conversation we have yet to have and will, I fear, now never have, given how little hold his slender volume has managed to retain on my memory and imagination.

He was small, prematurely bald and walked with a stoop he had developed to keep his gown from trailing on the ground. He had a distracted manner and a sense of bewilderment at the complexities which faced him every day as the man nominally in charge of an organisation the nature of which eluded not only him but all of us who worked within it. An Oxford college has variously been described as a social club, a dormitory, a debating chamber, a laboratory for social and academic experiments, a magnet and haven for the ambitious and the eccentric, a refuge from the outside world, an antechamber to a life of fulfilment. If St George's was some of those things all the time and all of them at some time, how could the Master possibly hope to navigate it through its constant external challenges, never mind its persistent internal redefinitions of its role? He listened and sought advice as best he could. He confessed that people baffled him, especially young people. Yet he made it his job to talk to every new entrant some time during their first term, and to remember their names and subjects thereafter. Unable to refuse any request, he had over the years, through a combination of poor judgement and chronically bad timing, found himself taking on administrative duties which others, including myself, had managed to avoid. Tutor on admissions, bursar, chair of numerous Senior Common Room committees, Dean of degrees. Finally, to his own surprise and not a little chagrin, he had, at the end of a labyrinthine process of nomination, selection and election which nobody seemed to understand, least of all he, assumed the prestigious title of Master. Electing a new pope is more transparent than this, he was heard to mutter when told the news.

'I just got back from the inquest,' he murmured as I walked into his massive, dimly lit room. His desk was piled high with files and loose papers. Several armchairs took up most of the floor space, hiding as best they could the worn patches of maroon carpet. He poured two glasses of sherry and sat down in an armchair which seemed to swallow him up, waving to me to sit down opposite.

'Accidental death?'

He frowned and shook his head. 'No. I'm afraid not. Suicide.'

My heart sank. My worst fears confirmed. I took too large a mouthful of sherry and coughed. I waited for him to elaborate but a further minute passed in silence. I would need to feed him questions, though I was in no fit state to do so.

'Was the coroner definite about it?' I asked at last. 'No question at all?'

'None at all. He was definite. You had no idea he was depressed?'

'The police asked me about that. Absolutely no idea. The contrary, in fact. He was… well, I would say things were looking up for him. He was shy and unimpressive at first. Struggled in his first year. Trying to find his feet, I suppose. It's often the way with those grammar-school types. They try so hard to meet the academic standards that they neglect to develop themselves in other ways. They have to catch up on coping with being independent, getting on with people from a different sort of background, people with more… polish, shall we say. The work often suffers while they're going through those adjustments. But his work had improved a lot recently. And he seemed to be more confident in himself. He was looking ahead, I would have said.'

'Grammar school, eh? Like you.'

'That's right.'

'He was from Liverpool, wasn't he?'

'That's right. Like me again.'

Yes, our backgrounds were strikingly similar, yours and mine. Yet we had never talked about it. Had I worried that you might have been reluctant? But it was up to me to find that out.

'Did he mention any plans for the future?'

'Plans? No. I never asked. Didn't seem the type for business or industry. Local government, perhaps, or the civil service. But we never talked about that. We don't normally discuss those things until their final year, when they start to give their futures some serious thought. Was there any mention of a suicide note?'

'None found. The coroner said he couldn't draw any conclusions from the absence of a note, not when the evidence in favour of suicide is as strong as that. They are not as common as is usually supposed. Notes, I mean. Not suicides. Though thankfully, they're not that…' He dried up.

'Were the parents there?'

'Just the father. I was going to ask you…'

My heart sank again. I was not good at coping with grieving parents. Not that I had any experience. But I knew I would not be. On those, for me, blessedly rare occasions which could be described as social, I could be relied on to fail to find the right words, or often to find any words at all. What if your father asked me for an explanation? How would he react when he found out how little I knew about you?

'The police have handed his room back to us,' he continued, 'though of course we're keeping it out of use for the time being. Major Max put his possessions into boxes. The father is calling next week to collect them. I was wondering if you would meet him, hand the boxes over, have a sympathetic word, all that sort of thing. I mean, you're the one who knew him best. Among the Fellows, I mean.'

There was a slightly accusing edge to his words. I should have known you better, he was implying, and he was right. I was totally ill-equipped for the role he had assigned me. But I could not deny the responsibility.

'How did the father seem, at the inquest?' I asked, after a few moments of unproductive reflection on how I would handle the meeting with him.

'He showed no reaction that I could see. He was smartly dressed, very dignified. I shook hands with him afterwards, had a few words, expressed my sympathy for his loss, usual vacuous words. But what else can you say? He just nodded. He must have still been in shock. He was the one who had to identify the body. Just imagine. My own son was here, ten years ago. When they do well like that, come to a place like this after all that hard work, you have so much pride and hope in them. Though you try not to show it too much, so as not to put too much pressure on them, you know. But you can't help being proud and indulging in the occasional dream about their future. And then for it all to end like this. And to have to see his body like that, lying there lifeless on a slab. I know they try to make it as presentable as possible but it must have been in a very bad way, after all that time in the water. I would have gone to pieces. But he still seemed to be in control of himself. Then he said...'

'What?'

'It was the only thing he did say. He said that his wife, Simon's mother, was not well and couldn't come. It was as if he were apologising for her absence. That was all.'

I was relieved. I said a silent prayer that your father would continue to control himself until after his meeting with me. Quiet dignity I might be able to cope with. A weeping father would be too much. A tearful mother would be preferable. I could arm myself in advance with a clean handkerchief to give her. You can't give a man a handkerchief to dry his eyes. You can't give a man a comforting touch. The Master sat quietly, looking vaguely into the distance. He had not dismissed me and I sensed he still wanted my company. But he had nothing more to say. He had already had too much of a dose of reality that day. It was up to me to pick up the thread.

'Going back to the verdict,' I ventured at last, 'what was it that made the coroner so sure? I mean, he fell into the water, so I heard, so it could have been an accident.'

'Did he drink?'

'Something else the police asked me. I have no idea.'

'Not whisky, as far as you know?'

'Whisky? Surely not. I can't believe any of them drink whisky. Beer or wine, perhaps. But whisky is for old codgers like us.'

He frowned. Before his nomination as Master he and I, while never friends, had known each other well enough for mutual teasing now and then, in the mild manner appropriate for academic circles. But since his elevation he had been forced to establish a barrier between himself and all such casual banter, one I had just thoughtlessly crossed.

'Speak for yourself, Alan,' he muttered.

'It's so damned expensive for a start. Then it's an acquired taste, one which I never acquired myself. Why do you ask?'

'The officer giving evidence at the inquest said there was an empty whisky bottle in the punt.'

'No doubt it was his punt?'

'None at all. The number was on it, and the college crest. He had booked it out himself, the one with that number. The police officer said they had found it tied up. Near Oak Walk, in the Parks.'

'I know the spot. Tied up, you say? Empty, with an empty whisky bottle?'

'Yes, that's what he said.'

There was a distinct note of irritation in his voice. Whatever it was he was expecting from me, it was not the need to repeat himself on tedious matters of detail.

'And the pole?'

He glared at me. It was a detail too far. But Pearson and the inspector had put the image of the pole in my mind, with their talk of how it was possible for the pole and punt to become detached, for the punter to fall in while attached to the pole. I was forming an image of the scene in my mind and with my habit of academic rigour I needed to know where to place the pole.

'It was mentioned. Laid out inside the punt. If you really want to know.'

So you were not punting at the time, not holding the pole, not in any danger of losing your balance. The inspector had told me none of that. You had punted to that spot, tied up, laid down the pole inside and… then what? Sat down to finish a bottle of whisky, to drink the whole bottle in one go if you had brought it with you unopened.

'I had asked Max about the booking system, so I could tell the coroner,' he went on, in a tone which suggested he had decided to humour my appetite for tiresome and irrelevant detail. 'The booking sheet for each day is placed in the lodge at nine o'clock. He could have booked it then or any time after, up to the moment he left, so long as nobody else had booked it. There was one of our students at the inquest. He had gone to the police with what he knew. Parnell by name. You won't know him. Maths, third year. He said he was at the punt house at the same time as Simon, with his girlfriend. He had booked his punt about half past nine that morning. He couldn't remember if anybody else's name was already on the sheet. He was getting ready to take his punt out. Then he noticed Simon. Simon was already on the river, pushing his punt away from the bank. Parnell noticed him because he was on his own. He couldn't see if Simon had anything with him. I suppose he would have stowed it out of sight. I'm referring to the bottles. He didn't know Simon well so he didn't call out to him. But it did strike him as a bit odd. The fact that he was on his own. You don't normally take a punt out on your own, do you? The pathologist said he had consumed enough alcohol consistent with his drinking a whole bottle.'

'Bottles?'

'Sorry?'

'You said "bottles"? Didn't you, just now? Was there more than one whisky bottle?'

'No, no. I'm talking about the other one. That was what really clinched it as far as the verdict was concerned. The pills.'

My stomach was already heaving, the taste of the sherry acid in my mouth. Now it lurched again.

'Pills?'

'Yes. Sleeping pills. Very strong tranquillisers. There was an empty chemists' pill bottle in the punt, one of those brown glass things. He must have swallowed the entire contents.'

'Who had prescribed them for him?'

'Nobody knows. The label with the chemist's name had been scraped off. It wasn't the college doctor. He was there at the inquest. Simon had not consulted him once since coming up. He said he would never have prescribed pills of that strength for anyone that young, at least never in that quantity. He would have referred him for counselling first, or for a psychiatric assessment if he thought it was really serious. Whenever he did prescribe pills like that it was always in very small doses so he could monitor the patient's reactions. It's a complete mystery. But what is not a mystery is his suicidal intent. No doubt about that. Terrible business. Terrible.'

He shook his head and relapsed into solitary thought. It was time for me to slip out and leave him to it. He would need to gather his thoughts and energies for what was to follow, the letter of sympathy to the bereaved parents and no doubt further meetings with them, the long meetings of the College Council to discuss what had gone wrong and ways to prevent it happening again. The press. And somehow he would have to find ways to lift the morale of the college, to restore its vitality and sense of purpose. It was no longer enough now for him to be the good committee man. He would have to lead and inspire, a role he had never sought and for which he knew he was not suited. But the Fellows and the students would be looking to him. Already, in only a week, he seemed to have aged by several years.

Whisky and pills. So you equipped yourself with those for your last journey. Easy enough for you to buy a bottle of whisky. But who prescribed those pills for you? Did you get them over a period or all at once? Surely not the latter, if the testimony of the college doctor is to be relied on. So how long did it take you to accumulate them? Weeks, maybe months. And why, while you were doing so, were you still writing carefully researched essays and noting down future assignments? And what was the cause of your apparent contentment? Had you reached your decision some time before, one which for reasons I will never know had finally brought you peace of mind? Was I wrong after all about your motives for the extra effort with your work? Was it aimed not at a better degree than expected but at deceiving me as to your true and already decided destination in life? And why had nobody, least of all me, the slightest intimation of your intention?

FIVE

Maximilian Harding, Major Max as he was known in the college, the head porter, had indeed been a major in the army, serving in Cyprus and Northern Ireland. He still bore a distinctly military air, underpinned by a well-trimmed moustache whose mottled hues clashed with the jet black of his full head of hair. On duty or off, he always wore a dark suit and tie when on college premises. In that respect he was far smarter and more impressive to an outsider than any of the Fellows. Shortly after his retirement from the army his wife and only son had been killed in a car accident. He never spoke of it himself, and I only learned of it during the course of a High Table conversation one evening. He had taken on the job of head porter to occupy his time, and, as he once confided to me, to keep in touch with the student life which his son, who had been sixteen at the time of his death, had not had the chance to enjoy. All the undergraduates were his surrogate sons now, he liked to say. He dealt with them in the firm but kindly way of a father. When they had problems, if their girlfriends were pregnant or if they were in trouble with the police over drugs, it was usually Max they went to first, even if the Dean, who was notionally responsible for discipline, had to be involved later.

When I told Max I had been allocated the task of handing over your possessions to your parents, he gave me the key, which he had been keeping under special security in a locked drawer in the lodge. In a solemn and almost whispering tone which he had clearly chosen with some care as the one most appropriate to the situation, he told me he had put everything into three cardboard boxes, which I would find stacked by the window.

I needed to climb a steeply winding stone staircase which narrowed with each turning. I had not been higher than the ground floor of any part of the college since my own undergraduate days, when I too had a room at attic level. I was out of breath by the time I got to yours. How had you managed to get all your stuff up here? I had, in my time, but then I had precious little to carry. Students nowadays have so much more. Several bouquets of flowers had been placed by the door, some already fading. So you were known and loved in college, more than I had realised. A notice was pinned to the door, barring entry to all except with the permission of the Master. Anyone claiming to have such permission was enjoined to obtain and sign for the key from the head porter.

I unlocked the room and entered, hesitantly. Simple furniture, narrow bed, desk and two chairs. One small lattice window, open, distant sounds of traffic and laughter. Still dizzy from my climb, I refrained from looking out onto the quad far below. An anglepoise lamp still on the desk, standard college issue. Three stout cardboard boxes neatly stacked by the window.

I opened the boxes gently, unable to resist the feeling that
I was committing a sacrilege. The accumulated possessions of
a lifetime. Not much when that life had only lasted nineteen
years. I had to look in case there was anything which might
be too traumatic for your parents to see. Like what? A letter
you were intending to send them telling them you hated them,
denouncing them for making your life a misery, for making you
want to end it? Nothing like that, thank goodness. There were
lecture notes, essays I had marked and returned. Specialist
books which I had recommended. Others which I had
definitely not. *One-Dimensional Man* by Herbert Marcuse.
The Divided Self by R D Laing. Poems of Yevtushenko. Less
popular reading than they would have been a few years
before, in the late sixties. Then they were all the rage among
the undergraduates, so one of them had told me, though I
had never been tempted to sample them myself. Maybe you
regretted having missed the ferment of those heady days,
when all established institutions and viewpoints were coming
under scrutiny.

A good thing, surely, that scrutiny. That is why the students
are here. We constantly tell them, as I told you, to think for
themselves now they are no longer at school and being led
by the hand through their exams. Back in those days I would
have found much the same sort of stuff on the shelves in every
undergraduate room if I had had the chance to look, heard
conversations about those books and the ideas they contained
every evening in hall if I had ever been in a position to listen
in. I had approved, as far as I could with my limited knowledge
and awareness. I could not be a part of it. It had all come too
late for me. But yes, I had to approve.

So were you, Simon, only indulging in nostalgia for
an era you had missed by just a few years, before the Tory
government and the looming economic crisis put an end to

student idealism? Or were you part of a movement to revive those ideals? If so, with whom did you share them? Had you discussed them here in this room, your excited, nervous chatter carrying on until the small hours?

What about the records? Some classical ones, fewer than I expected. Others were a surprise to me. They too spoke of the sixties at their height, when you would have been still at school. I had heard some of them, with little liking or understanding. Bob Dylan, Cream, the Stones (I had never liked them), recent Beatles (too far out for me, though I had always liked their early songs), Joni Mitchell, Leonard Cohen, Simon and Garfunkel. I supposed they would all soon end up in a rubbish bin, but that would be your father's decision.

I stole out of the room as if from a sanctuary and locked it carefully behind me.

SIX

My initial impressions of your father? Deliberate in his movements, studiously dignified, working hard to hide any appearance of nervousness. He wore a tweed suit with white shirt and dark green tie. No hint of black. That would have been too pretentious. When it came to the funeral he would be appropriately dressed, I had no doubt of that. He shook hands stiffly, bowing slightly before sitting down opposite us. He refused the Master's offer of a drink. The Master poured a whisky for himself and offered me one. Under the stress of events he had moved on from sherry to something a lot stronger. I was about to accept when I thought again about the bottle found in the punt. Undergraduates don't drink whisky. So how had you managed to get a whole bottle down? For a moment I sensed a nauseous swilling around my mouth and through my nostrils, the excess pressing upwards, urging to vomit free but held back by the slowly numbing senses. I shuddered and politely refused. He offered me a sherry instead, which I gratefully accepted.

We left it to the Master to start.

'Mr Harvey, I would like to assure you once again how deeply sorry we all are for your loss. It is our loss too. Simon was a credit to the college.' I had already briefed him not to say that you were an outstanding student. Your father might have known that was not really true. 'We will all miss him.'

Your father bowed again but said nothing. I was waiting for him to speak. Only then would I be able to assess the social and intellectual distance between him and you, to judge how he would react to the boxes and their contents. The Master continued in the same studiously controlled tones, softened to avoid any sense of intimidation but distant enough not to intrude on the emotional territory which was properly our visitor's. I wondered if he had been practising his words before a mirror.

'Mr Harris here was his principal tutor.' He glanced towards me. My prompt. I coughed.

'That's right, Mr Harvey. Simon was a pleasure to teach. He was a great credit to you, and of course to Mrs Harvey.'

He bowed again. Clearly, the only way he was ever going to speak was if I asked him a question. Knowing me, it would be a clumsy one.

'Were you at college yourself, Mr Harvey?' I ventured. The Master glared at me. Obviously not the right question.

Your father shook his head. 'No. I never went. Could have gone, but we needed for me to get a job. My own father died when I was very young. So just me and my mother. I worked in local government. Planning. Then the war came. North Africa for me. Could have been worse, I suppose. I enjoyed the company. Some great lads out there. Then back to local government. Not exactly exciting but steady.'

He spoke as stiffly as he held himself. No accent I could detect. He may have had one in the past but had worked hard to suppress it. A man in control of himself and his feelings. Especially feelings of loss. A man's man. A slightly wistful tone when he recalled his army friends. Nothing unusual about that for a man of his age and background. Nothing offensive or critical in his manner. If anything he was too polite, too understanding.

'Er... Mr Harvey, about your son's possessions,' I stammered, only too conscious of the shake in my voice. 'We have put them together and, if you like, we could help you... I mean, we have porters and between us we can get them from his room and help you put them in the car...'

The Master glared at me again, touching my foot with his toe. I had struck the wrong note again, sounding as if I were already trying to erase your memory from the college so we could all move on. God knows, I desperately longed to move on. Your father coughed and shuffled a little uncomfortably in his seat before replying.

'Actually, I was wondering... we only have a small car, and...'

'Would you like us to send them on? We could arrange that if it would suit you better.'

I avoided the Master's eye, sure that it would again be accusing me of hastiness. To my relief, your father showed no sign of taking offence.

'No, I didn't mean that, Mr Harris. It's very good of you to offer. I meant that his things would only upset his mother, when she saw them in the house. She's still trying to come to terms with what happened and if I returned with all that... What I mean to say is that it could really set her back. You understand? I was wondering, could you hang on to it here? Then if we decided we wanted it, or just maybe to come back some time and have a look through...'

The Master glanced at me, his eyebrows raised. I nodded.

'Of course, Mr Harvey. I have plenty of space in my room, here in college. We'll move the boxes there. They'll be safe. I'll respect their privacy, naturally. Then as soon as you want them, just let us know. In your own time.'

There was half a minute of heavy silence. Your father looked around the room, through the window, then down at the floor.

'What about the rest of the family?' asked the Master at last, realising I had exhausted my stock of questions. 'Is there anybody else you would like us to contact?'

He shook his head. 'There's only his brother. He already knows.'

The Master glanced at me. I shrugged my shoulders, very slightly so that your father would not notice. I was puzzled. I could recall no mention of your brother.

'Older brother?' asked the Master.

'Yes. Twenty-seven, now. A lawyer up in London. Very successful. Has his own business there. He'll be coming up to the funeral. It'll be very quiet. Just close family.' He stood up, his sudden movement taking us both by surprise. 'Well, thank you, gentlemen. Kind of you to see me like this. And to take care of his things. I'm sorry to impose on you like that, but his mother, you understand, she is in rather delicate health. She was already a bit that way before all this, and we have to be very careful, especially now. So I'll be off then and thank you again. Long drive ahead.'

We escorted him in silence to the car park. Passing groups of students fell back and into a respectful silence as we approached, guessing who the visitor was and the sad nature of his business in college that day. His car was a medium-size shooting-brake rather than the small car he had mentioned. Plenty of room in the back for all of your belongings with room to spare. Still, he had made his decision. The Master and I shook hands with him again, awkwardly, and waved to him as he drove off.

'Well, that could have gone a lot worse,' said the Master as we made our way back through the lodge. 'He doesn't seem to be blaming us for what happened. I mean, if we had had the slightest idea...'

'That's what is puzzling me,' I said. 'Not only did he not blame us, he never even asked if we had any idea why it happened or whether there were any signs, things that meant nothing at the time but might have done when looked at with hindsight. From the little I know about these things, bereaved people usually look for an explanation, even when they know in their hearts they will never find one. And I didn't sense any grief.'

The Master grunted. 'He's a typical Englishman of his generation. Holds his feelings in. Keeps things to himself. One day, it may all come tumbling out. I hope for his sake it does. In the meantime, you're the official curator of those boxes. All that's left of him now. I'll get one of the porters to take them over to your rooms.'

But there was one feeling your father had not tried to repress. His pride in the success of his elder son. His eyes had shone when he spoke of him. No images in his mind at that moment to compare with that which now haunted me constantly, of your bloated body wedged against the sluice gate. Was it fair to use pride in one son to suppress grief for another? But then who was I to judge how a bereaved parent should behave? I was not a parent and would never be one.

SEVEN

T he next day Max arrived in person at my door with the boxes, loaded on a trolley. I helped him to bring them in and stack them in a corner where in my normal line of business at my desk or my tutor's chair I would have no sight of them. As he stepped away I had to resist the usual impulse to salute, though I had narrowly missed national service and had no feel for the correct procedure. Even if I had made a clumsy attempt I was sure he would not mind. For his part, he stood upright, clicked his heels together, turned away and strode out of the door. His manner was even more military than usual, as if the situation required him, without being asked, to call upon and place at our disposal all his reserves of strength combined with deference.

I had another hour before my next tutorial. Slowly I sifted through the material in the boxes, more carefully than before. I opened a folder I had previously put to one side. It contained bank statements, a cheque book, two unpaid college battels bills. The bursar would have to be told about those. Your parents were liable, but now was hardly the time to approach them. Blushing at my own nosiness I looked through the bank statements. There was far more in your account than I would have expected any student to have. In my day I counted myself lucky to have a pound or two in the bank at any one time. So money worries could not have been the cause of your final act. One payment caught my eye. A quite substantial sum a year before, to a firm of London solicitors. Substantial to my eyes, anyway, and even more so to those of a student. The same surname. Your brother? Your father had told us he was a successful London lawyer. It would have been normal for him to help you out from time to time. So why a payment the other way round?

Of course your financial affairs were nothing to do with me. But somebody needed to sort all this out. The accounts would have to be closed and the outstanding sums returned to your family, after allowing for the outstanding liabilities to the college. Somebody needed to dispose properly of all your affairs. What was it called? Probate. Something like that. A lawyer would know. And it was obvious your father wanted nothing to do with anything like that.

I rang directory enquiries for the number of your brother's firm. A calm and efficient-sounding female voice answered and put me through right away.

'Mr Harvey? This is Mr Harris, from St George's College, Oxford. I am sorry to bother you. It is about Simon. I am, I mean I was, his tutor here.'

There was an uncomfortable pause. Did I have the right firm? Surely the call would not come as a surprise? But he did not seem to have any response ready. When it came it was businesslike, that of a lawyer rather than a brother, his default position, the one which came most naturally to him.

'Oh yes, Mr Harris. Well, what can I do for you?'

'First of all, I wanted to say how sorry we all are about what happened. It was terrible, and really so unexpected.' No response. I had to struggle on. 'He was doing well and seemed to be happy enough. Shows how little we can really know about what someone is thinking and feeling.'

I was rambling and I knew it. It seemed the right moment to stop and wait but still he said nothing. He was used to his callers being businesslike. So I had to get down to business.

'Well, the reason I am calling is… your father was up here yesterday. I suppose you know that. We told him we had all Simon's things here in boxes. I'm sorry, this may not be the time. But I suppose there are legal things to go through, you know. Processes. Your father asked us to hang on to it, so it is all here in my room. But there are personal things. Bank statements and the like. I was wondering, I mean, someone needs to sort it all out…'

He broke in at last, to my intense relief. 'Of course, Mr Harris. Thank you for taking the trouble. Yes, the old man is not really up to that sort of thing. He'll be happy to leave it to me. How much stuff is there?'

'Not that much. A few boxes.'

'How about I come up and collect them in the car. I could get away…' There were sounds of shuffling papers and a muffled conversation with the woman who had answered the phone, no doubt his secretary. 'Yes, I can get away tomorrow afternoon. Say, about four o'clock?'

'That would be fine. I'll arrange for a space to be reserved for you in the Fellows' car park. We can easily carry the stuff over from my room to there. Just around the corner.'

A wave of relief and fatigue washed over me. I would never have been comfortable with those boxes in my room, a constant reminder of a young life cut short. Now I could begin to forget, to concentrate on my other students and my researches. It was a tragedy but life had to go on.

But I was still uneasy. Like your father, your brother had asked no questions. Nor could I detect any more grief in his professional tones than your father had shown.

He tapped only once on my door before bursting in. I knew it was he rather than a student. They always wait after a nervous double knock for me to call out that they should enter. He had nearly reached my desk before I had time to rise out of the chair behind it. He offered his hand, smiling.

'Dr Harris. Pleased to meet you.'

'Er... plain mister, I'm afraid. Haven't got round to doing a doctorate yet.'

He seemed slightly taken aback.

'So what are you exactly?' His unbroken eye contact was unnerving.

'I'm a Fellow of the college. And tutor and lecturer in Anglo-Saxon studies.'

He shrugged his shoulders. 'I never understood how things work here. Never went to university myself. Straight from school to law school, then articles. Then set up my own business. So this is where the little swot learned it all, eh? Sitting at your feet?'

His relentless cheerfulness unsettled me even more than your father's reserve. 'Actually, he sat in that chair over there and I sat opposite. He read me his essays and we discussed them. That's how it works here. Why don't we sit down there now? Cup of tea?'

'No thanks. I'm a bit busy, actually. Always bloody busy. Need to get back.'

'Of course. I'll help you with the boxes. They're over there in the corner. So what was it you just called him? The little swot? Well, we have a lot of swots here. I suppose that describes me.'

He grinned. He was shorter than I expected, but that might have been because of his stance, which was slightly stooping with his shoulders forward, as if about to engage the front row of an opposing scrum. At the same time he smiled frequently as if to counteract the suggestion of threat in his posture. His whole demeanour seemed to be made up of elements which cancelled each other out.

'Oh, he didn't mind,' he said. 'It was a family joke. He was the school swot, top of the class or near. Always upstairs with his homework every evening. When he wasn't at church. He was there several times a week, serving on the altar. A pious swot.' He giggled. It was an edgy, high-pitched sound. 'Can you imagine? What a combination. Well, of course you don't need to imagine. You knew him. I wasn't a bit like him. I got through my exams but only by revising at the last minute. It wasn't quite revising. Often it was the first time I had looked at the stuff. Donkey's gallop. That was my style. That was a family joke as well. I was a lousy academic. But when it came to the real world, doing actual law, I found I was a natural. I have no idea how he would have managed in the real world. No offence to you types, you understand.'

'None taken. Was he really pious? I never knew that about him. He had no interest in religion as far as I knew.'

He shrugged his shoulders. 'Maybe he'd dropped it by the time he came here. We hadn't had much contact in recent years. So… did you have a good look through the boxes?' There was a slight hint of accusation in his words.

'No. Just enough to realise I could not hang on to them.'

'What's in them?'

'Books, of course. Essays. Records. Clothes. And the folder with his bank statements. I put that on top of the first box.'

'Fine. I'll look at that as soon as I get back to the office. Get rid of the rest of it later. Shall we get on?'

Between us we loaded his car in a couple of trips. It was a low-slung yellow Porsche with far more engine than luggage space. One of the boxes had to be placed on the passenger seat. He turned to shake hands, once more staring closely into my eyes.

'So there's nothing else you found? Nothing in his room, or anything his friends might have borrowed and given back to you? Everything is all here?'

He seemed suddenly to be suspicious of me. Did he really think I had pilfered from a deceased student? But then he was a lawyer. It was his job to suspect and ask questions until he was satisfied.

'Yes. You have my word. It is all there. His room was cleared out. I had nothing else of his in my possession. Of course if anything turns up...'

His smile was back again but this time it seemed forced.

'Oh, don't worry about it. Unless you think it's important. Like the number of his Swiss bank account.'

The laugh which followed was even less natural. His mask was beginning to slip. But what would he reveal beneath? Grief, anger, or just irritation at the disturbance to the flow of his life, the need to waste time in the company of a useless academic rather than a fee-paying client?

'I'll be off now, Mr Harris. Try and beat the rush hour traffic.'

A thought was forming in the back of my mind.

'Er, Mr Harvey, if you don't mind my asking... I suppose you'll be at the funeral?'

He screwed up his face for a moment, then pasted the smile back on.

'Probably not, I'm afraid. Very busy at the moment. Lot of new cases on. It's my own firm, you see. Different if I had a boss and could ask for time off. But when you're the boss... Why do you ask?'

'Your father said it would be a private affair. Just family. But…'

'You were thinking of going?'

I nodded. 'I thought someone from the college should be there. But I wouldn't want to intrude.'

'I wouldn't worry, old chap.' The unexpected note of false intimacy jarred on me. 'By all means turn up. They won't mind.'

'Have you got the details?'

'Sure. St Paul's Church, Crosby. That's in—'

'Yes, I know where that is. I come from quite near there.'

He frowned, perhaps struggling with the thought that an academic like me had actually come from somewhere rather than been bred in a laboratory within the college, and that in my case that somewhere was not so far from his own place of origin.

'Next Wednesday at noon. Catholic do. Mum was Catholic and so was he. Dad never was. It was a mixed marriage. I got out of all that stuff as soon as I could.'

'Me, too. I mean, I was brought up a Catholic. Not that far away. Bootle.'

'You and he had a lot in common then. More than could be said for the two of us. Well, I'll be off then.'

He jumped into the car. I waved and turned back to my room. Still no expression of grief. Not from the men of the family. Would your mother be any different? Was she grieving for all of them? How in her delicate state of health could she cope with that? I was surprised at my curiosity about the affairs of a family who had been total strangers to me until then. But somehow it would not let me go. And I knew it would compel me to attend the funeral.

EIGHT

Now I was on my way to visit our home town, Simon. For your funeral. I had not been there for many years. I took the train via Birmingham and booked into a hotel in the city centre. I do not own a car. I have never learned to drive. I don't suppose I ever told you that. Why should I? The occasion never arose. The next morning I took the local train to the station nearest to the streets where I had spent my childhood. After my trip down memory lane the same train service would take me on to where you lived, a little more suburban, more genteel, the sort of place to which my parents might have aspired, indeed which they might have achieved, if only... But I will come on to that. All in good time.

I had at least an hour to look around and see what if anything had changed. The answer was nothing as far as I could tell, except that streets were shorter and narrower and houses smaller.

My father was an officer in the Merchant Navy and absent from home for months at a time. I can barely remember what he looked like. He was tall, I suppose, but in the days of my early childhood every adult seemed intimidatingly tall. What else? Yes, the moustache, hiding any expression which might have shown in his face. Of his voice I have no memory at all. Men in those days were silent, a sign of strength. Chatter was for women.

My mother was much younger than he was, though I only realised many years later how much younger. For years she strove to be fashionable. The style of long plaid skirts and jackets curving from the shoulder to a high waist suited her full figure. But as time wore on those same clothes became drab and loose as she lost weight. Her face became prematurely lined with worry and the endless toll of household chores, the varnish of youth long since worn away. Worry about what? About things of which I knew nothing in those days. Debt, for one. The rent collector came every week, armed with slim red pocket book and fountain pen, bicycle clips always in place around his ankles, his imminent arrival announced by the deepening frown on my mother's face and the agitated movement of her hands as she sat at the table, counting the money. What else? Above all else, the approaching shadow of war.

Our street considered itself to be at least borderline respectable. The house was one of a terrace forming a boundary between a warren of streets leading into the city on one side and the rec on the other. The house front was narrow, but there was enough space between it and the pavement for a tiny garden, later given over to the growth of vegetables. The secret of the house, only discoverable by means of a tour of the interior or along a path that ran along the side, was its depth. There were no other houses at the back, so the builders had been able to stretch the downstairs enough to permit an extended dining room, a kitchen with massive cupboards which to my young eyes soared up to heaven, a parlour and a paved backyard with washing line and outhouse with coal bunker. Upstairs there were five bedrooms, including one I shared with my parents. I slept on a mattress behind a curtain. Beyond the wall of the backyard was the jigger, and beyond that the vast expanses of the rec.

"Rec" stood for recreation ground. I did not know that until I started school. I had already read enough to know that a wreck was the word for a ship which had sunk or run aground. I did not know why the space at the back of our house, a former reservoir grassed over and big enough for several football pitches, should bear that name. When our teacher at my first school asked us to write about our neighbourhood I described the space using the spelling I had always imagined. She read out what I had written to the class, spelling out the word as I had done, encouraging the hilarity which ensued. My nickname for months afterwards was "the wreck".

So that, surely, was the start of my lifelong search for precision, truth and accuracy. Did you ever wonder why I was so obsessed? It was because I had paid far too high a price too early for my carelessness with a single word.

My mother allowed me to explore the rec on my own but never to venture in the other direction towards the city centre. On the occasions I went that way with her, to the local shops or to visit one of her few friends, we saw children playing in the dusty streets, thin, dirty, in rags and without shoes. I asked why they too could not come to play in the rec. Because the grass was damp and they would slide on it in their bare feet, fall over and hurt themselves, I was told. Surely the hard pavements would hurt them even more, I responded. No, she told me, their soles were hardened, unlike mine. I felt soft, privileged, superior, unhappy. Despite their poverty I envied those children. They laughed and played games with each other. Tick, or hopscotch, or improvised football or cricket with whatever they could find, sticks, stones and pieces of plastic or rubber. I played on my own, the rec standing in for the Wild West I had read about in picture books, firing imaginary arrows or guns at my enemy, depending on which side I had chosen to be that day.

The house was always full of middle-aged ladies. Sisters, cousins and aunts perhaps, whose exact relationship to my parents I could never work out. I found out later that at least one had independent means. She was a widow and had inherited the proceeds from the sale of a small farm. Her comparative wealth did not seem to ease my mother's money worries. She was never to be found when my mother scurried about the house, raiding the various pots and jars used for saving coins in anticipation of the arrival of the rent collector or one of the local tradesmen who supplied on tick. As for the other ladies, I never knew if their dependence on my parents was real or if they too were just hangers-on. Without them my mother, grandmother and I could easily have managed in a much smaller and cheaper house. Nor did I know if the house had been specially chosen so it could accommodate the ladies, or if its size, a sign of more comfortable past times for my parents perhaps, had drawn them to it. They did not all live in all the time, but at any one time all the spare bedrooms were occupied, often multiply. My mother never tried to explain who they all were. I was told to address each one as "Aunt", followed by her first name, though I could rarely remember any of them correctly. The names were long and awkward on my still-developing tongue: Dorothea, Isabella, Stephanie, Anastasia. At mealtimes, the only occasions I was expected to say anything to any of them, they would laugh at my clumsy attempts with their names, then turn to each other once again for conversation carefully calculated to be above my head.

Then there was my grandmother. She occupied the corner seat by the fire, seated on a three-legged stool with a worn cushion which overlapped the edges, a thin grey blanket loose round her shoulders, her eyes fixed on the smoking, barely warm nutty slack which was always kept tightly packed to make it last, her constant companions the bronze coal scuttle and a pair of wood-carved concertina-style fireside bellows. As far as I saw with my own eyes she never moved, even taking her meals there. I knew she had her own bedroom, but by the time she went to bed I was long since in mine and she would always be up before me. She never spoke. She never looked my way, or anybody's way. It was hardly hyperbole to describe her as part of the furniture.

It was always with relief that I returned after mealtimes to my habitual solitude, outside on the rec or within the shadowy corners and recesses of the house, of which there always seemed to be more and more to be explored. My favourite room was the parlour, dark and damp with dripping whitewashed walls. It was my favourite because I would rarely be disturbed there, the life of the rest of the house usually stopping at the kitchen. If I heard anybody approaching, there was an easy escape route out into the yard and beyond. The parlour could serve as a secret cave with hidden treasures or a bandits' hideout, the mops and pails as swords and shields.

The parlour only came to life on Mondays, which was washday. My mother was in charge of the operation, sometimes helped by an aunt if one was available and in a helpful mood. The copper was built into a brick furnace, heated by coke, cinders, wood, old newspapers, anything combustible which was readily to hand. My mother, the whole front of her body covered with an apron, would agitate the washing in the copper with a wooden dolly peg, grunting and groaning, no doubt using the required level of violence to release the tensions which the week's frustrations had built up within her. Water aerated with harsh soap and soda flake suds would splash onto the floor and give out a clammy, chemical odour. Really dirty clothes were subjected to a special form of torture, being rubbed vigorously up and down a corrugated washing board. Then it was the turn of the mangle, a device which gave me nightmares after the aunt who had inherited the farm told me that in the countryside naughty boys would have their hands crushed between the wooden rollers to teach them a lesson. It stood sternly against the wall, heavily framed in wrought iron, waiting to swallow and regurgitate its weekly offering of dripping clothing, a tin tub placed beneath to collect the water. When it was in use I did not dare to go near it. I watched from a distance, awestruck. The huge, stiff wheel squeaked and wailed as it turned. Then the washing would be hung out in the yard to dry if the weather permitted, flapping high above my head, the line held aloft by a giant wooden pole. When the weather did not permit, which was much of the time, the clothes were hung on a ceiling dryer and airer, slats of wood which were hoisted up to the ceiling by pulleys.

The kitchen, which I would have liked to explore in depth but which was forbidden territory to all except my mother and certain aunts specially selected for their culinary skill, or more likely for an ability to lay the table efficiently, was stacked with pots, cans and jars, from some of which an exotic mix of stale odours rose. Their labels were faded and those of metal spotted with rust. None to my knowledge was ever opened, if indeed that was still possible, or used in the preparation of food. I could only assume they had come with the house and were still there as a result of the general embargo on the disposal of anything which might at some time "come in handy", to use my mother's favourite expression. At the side was a gas stove and coke boiler combination. Cooking was a long and exhausting process, judging by the hours my mother spent there and the state of her apron when she emerged. But the effort seemed out of all proportion to the result. Over-boiled potatoes were always the central item, typically with corned beef and watery canned peas and carrots. As rationing increasingly dominated the lives of my mother and those aunts who sometimes helped with the shopping, it became the main and in time the exclusive topic of conversation.

It was a time and place of drab greyness, in the food, in my clothes and those of the other occupants of the house, in the furniture, the streets, the grimy windows. Even the rec was grey. Its worn patches of grass were never given a chance to recover from the rough and tumble of children's play. When rain clouds were not covering the sky, a haze of smoke from the riverside factories and warehouses would drift in to take their place, sometimes congealing into a choking smog.

I was twelve when the bombs came. The port docks and warehouses were the targets, but streets less than a mile away from ours were sometimes hit, the fires ravaging the sky, the sirens wailing like demons erupting through the broken ground. At those times, and only then, the chatter of the aunts ceased. The windows had already been covered with heavy curtain material for the blackout. We took up our positions in the dining room. My grandmother shuddered into a semblance of life. She still sat by the now extinguished fire, but when the sound of the bombs came she put her cushion on her head and whispered repeatedly, 'Jesus, Mary and Joseph.' Nobody considered going to a shelter. The nearest was too far away for my grandmother, either to walk or be carried. We were not in pitch dark. A couple of battery torches were placed on the floor, allowing some faint shafts of light at ground level, their glass covers removed to avoid reflection. I crouched in the corner, my hands not over my ears but my eyes. It was that dim light I feared far more than the sound of the bombs. It specked the frozen features of my mother and the aunts with patches of spectral yellow. In the nightmares which would inevitably follow when I eventually fell asleep I found myself trapped in a vault, those motionless, faintly glowing bodies turned to statues, which later would start to move and approach me, emitting groaning sounds, bony fingers pointing at me and summoning me to hell.

My father was away, of course. His ship ploughed a dangerous furrow back and forth across the Atlantic, escorted by navy warships and hunted by submarines. A year into the war we received the news that his ship like so many others had been sunk with the loss of all crew. I knew him so little that I barely reacted. My mother's expression only hardened all the more. If she felt grief there was no time to indulge in it. Difficult decisions had to be made and the aunts were ready with their proposals. They concerned me. I had to be sent out of harm's way.

The day after my thirteenth birthday I was on the station platform, crammed into a stiff new school uniform. My mother could never have afforded it. The aunt of independent means had at last put her hand in her pocket. Now that same aunt was ready to put me on the train and see me off. The noise and the smell of burning cinders and steam invaded all my senses. My mother had not spoken a word that day. She had seen me and the aunt onto the bus and turned away, shaking her head. It was my last memory of her. My aunt, in recognition of the responsibility which had been placed on her, was dressed in her best outfit usually reserved for Sundays, a heavy green overcoat with matching hat and gloves. She was in no more of a mood for a farewell than my mother had been. She had a task to perform and that was to ensure I was on that train when it left.

I called out to her as the train door shut behind me, desperate to leave the impression of one who had shared their hard times and understood what they had gone through and had still to face, who was now grown up and, in principle at least, the sole surviving man of the family, who was ready to face the future with all its cares and responsibilities, who was capable of respect and courtesy towards his elders. 'Goodbye, Aunt...' I could say nothing further. I had forgotten her name. So much for my new-found adulthood. She had already turned away. For a moment she paused and nodded, her hat bobbing precariously. The danger to the hat was made much worse by jets of steam from the engine, so she put her hand to it but still did not turn round. Then she strode off.

NINE

So why am I telling you all this, Simon? I am not expecting pity. Many had it far harder than we did in those times. We were not poor, though my mother would have had fewer money worries if our spare rooms had been let to paying lodgers instead of given over to the aunts. Is it to show you how different our backgrounds really were, that despite our both being brought up as Catholics and coming from the same part of the world we never had anything in common so it would have been pointless for me to try to reach out to you beyond the defined bounds of our student-tutor relationship? We were separated by time and social change. Your world of youth, hope and freedom heralded the end of the one I had known at your age, of stoic pessimism and self-repression. Or am I trying to explain why I never tried, justifying the distance I kept between the two of us because distance was all I knew?

I watched the arrival of the coffin and the mourners from the other side of the street, then crossed over and slipped into a pew at the back. The church was small and bright, its full-length strips of abstract stained glass designed to catch and magnify the light. So different from the shadowy temple of guilt and fear where my mother had taken me every Sunday to pray for my sins and plead for redemption. The priest's appearance, plump and smiling, suggested a warm and comfortable lifestyle rather than one of penance and self-sacrifice. His sermons would never reek of fire and brimstone. Yet a suicide, a mortal sin according to Church doctrine, had to be a tricky subject for any priest, however sympathetic. How would he tackle it?

There were only three mourners apart from myself, all at the front to the right of the coffin. Your parents sat closest to the aisle. As she turned her head towards the coffin I saw that your mother wore a wide-brimmed hat from which black lace veils fell on either side like partly closed shutters. From what I could see of her face her lined features were set hard. Her eyes stared as if into a void. Your father did not stir. Next to your mother an elderly lady sat in quiet dignity. An aunt, surely. There are always aunts. I had learned that from a very early age.

The sermon began.

'Dearly beloved, a service for the departed is always a mixed occasion.' His voice was soft and musical, reminding me of the rural Ireland I had never seen but which some of my teachers had wistfully described. Your parents sat close to each other as if propping each other up, facing straight towards the altar. No movement. No discreet raising of a tissue to a moist eye.

'There is grief, of course,' continued the priest. 'But also joy. Joy when we can celebrate the fact that one of the faithful has been called to his Saviour's side, especially if the call comes as a blessed relief at the end of a time of pain and suffering, and where the life which has ended has been long and fulfilling.

But when the body which housed the departed soul was young and full of promise it can be hard to find a measure of joy to make up for the all too understandable grief. Simon's life was indeed full of promise. I knew him well. As a boy he served me and my fellow priests here on this altar for some years, always punctual, always respectful, always attentive to detail. He had patience, too, a gift with which I have to say he was better endowed than I. Often when I was moved to be cross and irritable out of all proportion to the cause it was his gentle, understanding smile which brought me back to myself. At school he was a diligent student, the reward for his efforts being a place at Oxford University, an achievement of which his parents were justly proud.

'But the shadows of adolescence, which visit us all but from which most of us mercifully and with God's help emerge with time, can fall even in the most beautiful and congenial of places and in the most supportive of company.'

I caught my breath at those last words. I glanced up at him. No, he was not looking at me. He was skilled and practised in avoiding individual eye contact. His eyes took in the whole pew area, as they would always do at his Sunday sermons, even though on this occasion most of the pews were empty. He had not intended his words for me. He had no idea who I was. Still I felt them cut into me.

'In Simon's case, the shadows, sadly, did not lift. They gathered and took possession of him. Nobody knew. Nobody even suspected. He was not the first young person nor, tragically, will he be the last of which this is true.'

He cleared his throat. 'I must come now to the most difficult and painful part of this address. I would be failing in my duty as an ordained priest if I omitted to mention, here before the Blessed Sacrament as well as before the deceased's mortal remains, a deeply uncomfortable truth. But I hope, after I have stated that truth, to find some cause for comfort in the hearts of those who have come here to mourn his passing.

'Simon was a good Catholic, devout and observant, during all the years I knew him. He departed this life as a result of his own actions. Let me not mince words. He killed himself. He committed suicide. The Church teaches us that killing is a mortal sin, and that applies as much when the killing is directed at the self as at another. So much we know. But there is much we do not know and can never know about the exact circumstances of Simon's departure. There are two possibilities as to what might have happened, either of which would be enough to turn away the wrath of our Saviour and lead Him instead to hold out the hand of welcome to Simon in Paradise.

'The first is this. The darkness and the weight of the clouds which enveloped his young mind were such as to deprive him of all reason, to blind him at that time to the reality of the Christ he had always known and loved, to lift from him any responsibility for his actions at that moment of the profoundest darkness.'

I grasped at his words, desperate to believe them. At the same time I pushed them away. Were you really deprived of reason for all the time it took to plan your death, to gather together the means to accomplish it, to determine all the necessary ways to deceive us as to your intentions? If the priest had known more he would surely not have said those words. But perhaps he did know and was merely finding ways to comfort.

'The other is this. This much we do know, that his death was not sudden or violent but slow. Not slow and painful, but a progressive numbing of the senses, a gradual farewell to this world and its trials, trials which to him then appeared to be insurmountable.'

So he did know something of the manner of your death. Implicitly he had already rejected the first of his two possibilities. I knew what the second would be. Already I doubted it. Would your faith, would anybody's, be strong enough to survive so long beneath such heavy and prolonged despair only to re-emerge in triumph just at that final moment?

'We do not know how long that process of sliding into unconsciousness lasted. But time enough for repentance, for a last Act of Contrition, for a final prayer for forgiveness? Surely that was the case.' He paused to let his words sink in.

'If we cannot know yet we can believe. This is what Christ teaches. That is what faith is. And my faith, my profoundest belief, is that Simon is today with his Saviour in Heaven. He was young, his life blameless, his heart and his deeds dedicated to others. How many of us can say so much of those whose presence in Heaven we would not for an instant question? How many of us can say so much of ourselves, who aspire one day to be worthy of that presence when we too are called?

'So let us find some joy today amidst the grief for a life cut short so far before its time. Let us celebrate who Simon was and how he lived his life. Let us hold the image of that life before us as an example and a beacon. Thanks be to God.'

I left before the end of the service, watching from the same concealed spot as before as the mourners and the coffin came out, the priest reciting familiar Latin prayers, your parents stiff and dignified, your mother still with the same mask she had worn in the church. Your aunt, if such she was, followed at a distance, crow-like, head bowed, shoulders shrouded in a black scarf. They all moved around the corner of the church towards the cemetery at the back. I watched and waited. Though all are welcome in a church the graveside ceremony is strictly for family.

When they emerged and the family had driven away, enveloped in the reassuringly upholstered interior of the black funeral car, the priest stood outside and waved. As he turned back towards the church door I walked up to him, a knot of nervousness collecting in the pit of my stomach as I recalled the fears instilled into me during my childhood years. Priests were the representatives of God on earth. Their authority came directly from Him. They were the anointed successors to the Apostles of Christ. They were His agents in the sacraments, in the transformation of bread and wine into His body and blood, in the forgiveness of sins. Many had acquired an aura of unapproachability to go with their appointed role. But this one had to be different, though still meriting the hallowed form of address.

'Thank you, Father. That was a lovely service. I'm Mr Harris. I was Simon's tutor at college. I kept in the background. In the church, I mean. I know it was just for family, but I felt I had to come.'

He smiled and shook my hand warmly.

'Good of you to come, my son. You could have come to the grave. Nobody would have minded. In a sense you were family.'

'Not really. I should have known him better.'

He raised an eyebrow. 'Seen what was coming? Please don't torment yourself with that thought. I have conducted services for young people who left us long before their time. Nobody ever saw it coming. Not even their closest friends or family members.'

'If I might say so, I thought your sermon struck just the right note, Father. Such a difficult and sensitive subject for a Catholic. Suicide, I mean.'

His smile invited me to continue. He knew from long and compassionate experience that people who need to talk to a priest for whatever reason rarely come straight to the point.

'Father, could I ask you something? I have spoken to the father, and the brother. He isn't here. He told me he couldn't make it. I haven't met the mother yet. I was wondering, is their reaction typical?'

'How do you mean?'

'So little obvious grief. His father is very stoic. His brother tried to make light of it all. And his mother, well, from what I could see she seemed a bit distant.'

'Typical, maybe not. Unusual, by no means. People have different ways of coping. I have seen them all. Some only let their grief emerge much later.'

'You said how religious Simon was. I never knew. Where did he get that from?'

'From God, of course. But I think I understand your question. You mean did he follow the example of a family member? His mother was a very strong Catholic. I have met his father and we got on well enough. But he is the staunchest atheist I have ever met.'

'You said his mother was a strong Catholic. Has that changed?'

He paused, clearly wondering how much he could say without breaching a priest's duty of confidence. He decided to continue, perhaps sensing he could trust me as one who like him had had a sort of pastoral duty of care for you.

'It's very strange,' he said at last. 'It changed from the moment Simon came here to serve on the altar. Before that, she and Simon always came to Mass together on Sunday and Confession every Saturday. Not the brother. He was never interested. Took after his father in that respect. But when Simon started to serve on the altar, which meant him attending several times a week and at least twice on Sundays, she stopped coming to the church altogether. I never saw her. She never came to Confession any more. I have visited her from time to time in recent years but she never wanted to talk about it. I respected that, of course.'

'But she asked you to conduct a Catholic service for him.'

'No. No, she didn't. Strangely enough, that was her husband. He said he thought she would approve. Apparently he couldn't talk to her about it. You see, she is not very well these days. Nothing physically wrong. But in her mind she is not well. She is becoming very forgetful. So Mr Harvey had to make all the decisions about the funeral.'

So you had found a replacement mother. Holy Mother Church, as it is often called. Very appropriate in your case. But what about her? She had sent you to serve on the altar at the very moment she had apparently lost her own faith. Was that to make up for the loss? If indeed you had given up your own faith at college, as your brother suggested, or at least your habit of observance, was it because you were no longer needed as a surrogate?

No, it won't do. Surrogacy, I mean. Not in this case. I attended church regularly as a child. I went to a Catholic boarding school during the war. I know the rules. You have to take the sacraments in person. You cannot send a delegate. Not even the Pope can do that. You can take Communion only for yourself, after confessing only your own sins. Your sins could not stand in place of hers or subsume them. She must have known that.

TEN

I had not thought to send flowers to your funeral. The idea of going back to the church to ask the priest where the grave was only came to me as I was on the train back to Oxford. But there was somewhere I could lay a bouquet. Nobody would see me. Or if they did, they would not understand why I was placing it just in that spot.

I was wrong about that. I was seen, by someone with the same idea.

I had gone to the mill and was staring down into the water before the sluice gate. The early afternoon sun beat down. I cursed my jacket and tie. But I possessed no casual wear, for that or any other season. A hot, dry early summer had followed the spring rains and the millstream was low and sluggish, the side walls damp and mossy. A floating dam of rotting wood and leaves had built up before the sluice gate and bobbed gently on the surface, stirred only by the slow leakage of water beneath. A stale, dank odour rose heavily to my nostrils, not even a flutter of breeze to disperse it. The elements of air and water had borne your body to that place and held it there and now they were exhausted.

I had approached the mill along the path from the Marston Road. Nobody had followed me. I saw it straight away. The fresh bunch of wild flowers laid on the ground directly above the gate had not been tied. They had been picked specially. Ahead of me on the Mesopotamia path a tall man was walking away, his hair long and flowing. Despite the heat he wore an open coat of black leather, almost ankle-length. He had nearly reached the first trees by the side of the path when on an impulse I ran after him and called out.

'Excuse me.'

He stopped and turned round. Not yet a man. Not yet old enough to have learned that a man does not cry. It was a shock to see his tears. But I felt something else at the same time. Relief. You had died and nobody had yet seen fit to cry. Now at last someone was crying. I knew it was he who had left the flowers. Though I had to ask, if only to explain why I had addressed him.

'I'm sorry, I just wondered... Was it you who left those flowers?'

He was thin with high cheekbones and a fair to pale complexion. The open coat revealed faded jeans and a loose brown pullover. His scarf was loose over his shoulders in the studiously casual manner affected by undergraduates. He looked pointedly at the shop bouquet I still held clutched in my hand.

'It's all right,' he said. 'You can leave yours as well. I'll come back with you. If you want.'

His voice had long since grown out of the fractured tones and pitches of the break, but it would be some years before it found the cynical heaviness of adult certainty. It had that unique musicality of adolescence, full of the wonder of thoughts and questions adumbrated for the first time. I had heard it so often in my students. But only at that moment when he spoke did I acknowledge that it was one of the few joys and privileges of my life, to hear even the crudest of essays and the clumsiest of questions expressed in tones of youthful curiosity and sheer excitement in discovery. I knew I could never find such moments again within myself but through my students I could relive them. Through them and, until you decided to leave us, through you. The voice of my new acquaintance reminded me of you, with an acute stab of pain and loss which made me want to cry out.

Though his voice was different from yours. Anonymously public school, impossible to place in any one locality. From the moment you had first come for interview, and despite the little you had said, I had recognised your slight accent as native to my own place of origin, though I had never adopted it myself. Why then had I not told you that I too came from there, not found common ground with you at least on that score if on no other? Was I ashamed of my origins, proud to have risen above them? In other words, was I an insufferable snob? Somehow there was time for all these thoughts to race through my mind before I nodded and tried to smile.

'Yes, thank you. I'd like you to join me. I was going to say a quick prayer. Not that I can remember many. I can just about manage an *Our Father*.'

We walked back slowly. I placed my flowers next to his and recited the prayer slowly and quietly. He joined with me in the final amen. We then turned back in the direction he had been following when I had called out to him.

His pace was naturally leisurely and I struggled to match mine to it. Over the years I had affected a way of bustling about the quad and along the streets which must, when I think about it, have looked comically absurd. For some reason I had thought it appropriate for an academic always to appear to be pressed for time, though in truth my way of life rarely called upon me to hasten anywhere. He seemed in no hurry to talk either, but neither did he appear to resent my unexpected company.

'I was his tutor,' I said after a few minutes. 'I'm Mr Harris.'

'Ah yes. I thought you might be. He spoke a lot about you. He admired you a lot.'

'And you were a friend of his?'

He nodded.

'Are you an undergraduate? I don't recognise the scarf, I'm afraid.'

'Yes. St Cuthbert's.'

'What do you read?'

So formal, that question, yet so casual, so common. He might take it either way, and either way be offended and withdraw, undoing the little we had achieved so far to make contact. I had simply asked him what he read. At Oxford undergraduates don't study, they read. As if it were all easy, something they take in their stride, in between more important matters. There are always some for whom it is indeed like that, or so they make you think. But you were not one of those. You studied. Hard. But what about your friend?

'History. Second year.'

'Very good.'

I was perhaps showing too much enthusiasm. For all I knew he might hate his chosen subject. He wouldn't be the first.

'Did you go to the funeral?' he asked, casually.

'Yes. It was very quiet. I'd been told it was family only so I kept a low profile. I didn't speak to anyone.'

And nobody was crying. Unlike him.

'I didn't know where or when it was. I didn't know the family.'

'Neither did I. I met his father, briefly, after it happened. Then I met his brother. He came to collect his stuff.'

He stopped, suddenly. I had already gone on a few paces before I realised. I turned round. He wore a slight frown, as if trying to take in the significance of what I had just said, though I had intended nothing more than the conversational padding at which I was so unskilled.

'His brother? He's got all his stuff now?'

'Yes. His father didn't want it. His brother agreed to take it and sort out his affairs.'

He started to walk again, nodding slowly.

'His affairs. Yes.' He muttered the words to himself. Then he looked up with a sort of wan smile.

'I suppose that was it,' he continued. 'What we had just now. Our own funeral service. Your flowers and mine. The prayer. Very intimate. Much better than any church business.'

'Yes, much better. Can I ask you this? Were you close friends, the two of you? Did you know him well? I was wondering...'

'...if I knew what was going to happen? No. It was a surprise. God, that sounds so weak. A shock, I mean. A terrible shock.'

'Yes, to me as well. To all of us. I don't know if he talked about his work much. But he was making very good progress. I was thinking of nominating him for an honorary scholarship. He was a quiet sort, of course, but he seemed happy enough. More than when he first came up. It was so... out of the blue.'

'I read about the inquest, in the *Oxford Mail*. He drowned. Fell in while under the influence of drink and pills. They didn't say what drink or what pills. He didn't drink. A glass of wine every now and then, when we could afford it. We would buy a bottle between us, once a term, make it last. And he never took drugs. I'm sure of that.'

'I can tell you what I know.' Why not? His tears deserved it. 'The Master was at the inquest and he told me. It was whisky. Nearly a whole bottle. And the pills were tranquillisers. Nobody knows where he got them.'

He stopped again and stared at me. 'Whisky? He never drank that. He once told me he couldn't stand the stuff. Even the smell of it made him want to puke.'

'The other odd thing is that he didn't leave a note.'

'They usually do, don't they? Suicides, I mean.'

'Often, but not always. That's my understanding.' That was what the Master had heard, and what he had told me.

He had stopped at a point where the path branched off to the left, towards some tennis courts and a car park. Further away were the low-rise buildings of his college, modest glass-sided cubes strung out alongside the riverbank and in the fields between the river branches. I knew the college slightly. I had been invited there to dine at High Table a couple of times. It was an open, smiling place, completed only a few years before, looking spiritedly to the future, making only a token nod to the past in its modernist take on the traditional layout of quads, staircase and hall, the buildings set apart so that air and space could circulate. It was not dominated by walls. No ghosts had yet had time to people it with ancient memories. It would not have suited me at all.

'I go this way,' he said, after an awkward moment of silence. 'My college is just over there, and I'm a bit late for a tute. It was very nice meeting you.'

'And you. Perhaps we could meet again, for a sherry in my room. Or afternoon tea, if you prefer.'

Sherry or tea. Standard Oxford rituals, the invitations made more often than not out of politeness rather than in the expectation that they would be taken up. Was that how he would take it? He surely would, unless I added some real intent to my hollow-sounding words.

'I know it must be painful for you,' I went on, a little too urgently, but he was already beginning to walk away. 'Only perhaps it would be good to talk some more. About Simon, I mean. I know I would like to, if you wouldn't mind.'

The pale smile again, a little broader this time.

'Yes, I would like that.'

He turned away with a casual wave. Now he was running, with an effortless energy. I called after him but I had no chance of catching him. I had not even asked him his name. So I would have to wait until he chose to contact me. But what if he did not? He would have many friends, numerous distractions to take his mind off the tragic death of one of them. Young people are resilient to the point of callousness. They have to be. Their whole *raison d'être* is their future. They can move on from calamities in the same way as they put random incidents behind them. They move on because they have no choice. The death of his friend was a tragedy, but it would already be starting to fade, the flowers and tears of today to be followed by the joys and hopes of tomorrow. As for his brief meeting with a solitary bachelor don, that would be forgotten already.

But I did not want to forget. I was aware of an ache in the pit of my stomach through which I struggled to breathe, a desperate need to see him again and talk to him. Without realising it he had with all the careless cruelty of youth stuck a knife into my heart. Why, for God's sake, had I not asked him his name?

I followed at a fast walking pace to the entrance of his college, past the porters' lodge and into the quad. Groups of chatting students and tourists. No sign of him. I walked round the perimeter. Sixteen staircases in all, a dozen rooms on each. He could be in any of them. I looked in the library, the dining hall, the Junior Common Room.

No sign.

ELEVEN

I received his handwritten note two days later.

I was puzzled at first. The writing, clearly and
sensually shaped and meticulously punctuated, was
unfamiliar. None of my students wrote like that, nor any of
my donnish colleagues. The latter took a perverse pleasure
in being barely decipherable. There was no address at the
top nor signature at the end. The note asked if I would meet
him in the chapel of my college the following day at four
o'clock, when there would be choir practice for evensong. He
would watch and wait for me to go in and he would join me.
It would be as if we had both gone in by chance to listen to
the music.

I was delighted and taken aback at the same time. Now I
could have no doubt he was aware of the impression he had
made on me. My defences had crumbled the moment we had
met. He knew he did not have to remind me of our encounter.
More than that. He knew I would have thought of nothing
else since. He held all the cards. He was setting up our next

meeting in a mysterious, even melodramatic, way according to his own purposes, whatever they were, and I could not refuse. Even his name was still his secret.

I have a confession to make, Simon. I rarely visit our college chapel, or any other. Perhaps I associate them too much with painful memories of my church at home. But that should not have stopped me accepting that invitation you sent me to a concert you had organised in our own chapel. Something else did. Some engagement of so little importance that I cannot now even recall it. I should have gone to your concert. I would have heard you play. Now I never will.

I had no choice but to sit there and wait. I looked about me with the eyes of a tourist. It is not cavernous, unlike some in the larger colleges. Rather it is squat, just about managing to accommodate four double stained-glass windows on each side set in heavy stone recesses behind the choir stalls, leaving room only for a few pews at the back for congregation and visitors. Reaching across the roof space is a network of wooden beams in rhomboid shapes, which give the impression of being a temporary scaffold rather than of having held the roof there for centuries. The geometry of the wood gives the upward-craning visitor the impression that the tops of the walls are about to fold in on each other, fortunately only an unintended *trompe l'oeil* effect.

The crowning glory, if one can speak in such terms of a building which is distinctly modest in aspiration and achievement, is the organ loft, taking up half the wall above the entrance and accommodating an ambitious array of gleaming pipes more suitable for a much larger space.

An incident from very early in my undergraduate days may have contributed to my reluctance to visit the chapel since. This should interest you, with your musical background.

One day I might have got round to telling you about it. It was my first evening in college. I was making my way through the gloom of the deserted quad, looking for my staircase, when a mighty sound burst forth from the open chapel door and enveloped me, the vibrations of the lower notes seeming to come from below the paving, the higher notes from a celestial orchestra above. Forgetting about my room, I fumbled my way inside. The interior was in total darkness apart from a patch of light in the organ loft. I recognised the music, Bach's *Fantasia and Fugue in G Minor*. I sat down in the choir stall, close to the door and out of sight. Whoever was playing expected to be alone and would surely resent an intruder. I slipped out quietly before the end of the piece. Later that week I met the college organ scholar and started to congratulate him on his playing. Before I could go on, he denied having been in the college that evening, nor was he aware of anyone else who could have been there in his place. He had his own explanation, which he conveyed to me in hushed, awestruck tones. The organ was a recent replacement for its predecessor, which had fallen into disrepair. The piece was one which Bach liked to play on the many occasions he was asked to test a new organ. So it must have been the ghost of Bach who had paid us a visit to try out the new instrument and give it his seal of approval. Certainly I was ready to believe that the sound which had overwhelmed me that night had come from the master himself.

This time the chapel gave no aura of being haunted nor having ever been. There was some light from the windows and there were a few whispering visitors with cameras. The organ was not in use this time, though the music was again by Bach, his motet, *Jesu meine Freude*, for choir *a capella*.

I was aware of someone slipping into the space next to me and picking up one of the missals which had been left there. He had brought a small leather briefcase. He looked around, then opened the case and took out a foolscap envelope. Passing it with his left hand under the missal he dropped it into my lap, just brushing my hand.

'Don't open that, whatever you do,' he said, not looking at me, leaning forward towards the loft whence the sounds of the choir came. He spoke just loudly enough for me to hear him over the music. 'I want you to keep it safe for me. I need someone to trust, someone who knew him. He trusted you so I'm doing the same. Can I come and see you? Not like this. Normally, as if you were giving me a tute or something. I can't say any more now, but I'll tell you about it then. Sorry to be mysterious but I think someone may be following me.'

There was a break in the music. The conductor was asking for more tone from the sopranos. My heart was pounding and my mouth ash-dry. What was going on? Was he really in danger? Or was it just paranoia in an overheated young imagination, one rendered desperate and vulnerable from the death of his friend and the sudden end of one of the certainties of youth, that life went on forever? I could not blame him for overreacting to an event which had brought him far too soon face to face with his own mortality. Or was I the one in danger, from a cruel hoax he had decided to play on me, sensing he had me at his mercy? Perhaps he had friends outside in whom he had confided, who would be waiting to hear his report and to laugh at the readiness with which an eccentric old don had fallen prey to their youthful wiles. Or maybe he had a crueller plan to which only he was party, to break my heart for the sheer joy of it, for the exercise of a power I had unwittingly given him, for no other reason than that he could. If he even slightly suspected how badly I needed his company, the temptation for one with all the power of youth and beauty at his disposal could be overwhelming. But far better any of that than that we should not meet at all.

'Come to me for a tutorial,' I whispered at last. 'Can you make tomorrow at eleven? Wear your gown and bring an essay. Any essay.'

'I'm not too hot on Anglo-Saxon lit, I'm afraid.' He still looked ahead but I sensed his smile, heard the relaxation in his tone. His words were still safely camouflaged by the echo of Bach's counterpoint. 'I've heard of *Beowulf* but that's all. Would something on the Peterloo Massacre do? I got a beta plus for it.'

'That would do nicely. What's your name?'

'It's on the envelope. Alban. Alban Knight. As in of the Round Table.'

'Look forward to seeing you tomorrow, Alban.'

I turned towards him, ready to let him interpret the gesture and my words in whatever way he chose, whether as his victory or my surrender, but he had already stolen away. He had replaced the missal. I picked it up, feeling the warmth of the leather cover where his hand had caressed it. Then I felt my hand where his had brushed it in handing me the envelope.

The secret package, thin and light. What part did that have to play in his plan? Whatever it was, I would obey. I would hide it and not dream of opening it.

TWELVE

He did not turn up for his supposed tutorial. Perhaps the joke had worn thin already. He and his friends had had a laugh about it and then decided that it was time to move on.

Yet his anxiety had seemed genuine enough. If he was acting, he was very good at it. And he had come to me from a place of grief of whose sincerity I had no doubt. He had placed his flowers not at your door with the others but at the spot where your body was found, not expecting anyone else to have the same idea at the same time. His tears had been real. They had started well before he realised he was not alone.

I waited a few days before swallowing my pride and sending him a note at St Cuthbert's. I told him that if the time we had arranged had proved inconvenient he was welcome to suggest another. I left it at that. If there was still the hint of a prank in the air then I needed to be careful to give nothing away in writing that could be exploited to my disadvantage.

Another week passed and still no word from him. I thought of the envelope I had locked away in the cupboard where I kept my personal papers. Were they part of the joke or did they really contain a secret which could harm him? He had said he trusted me as you had trusted me. But you had not trusted me enough to tell me about the dark thoughts which had driven you to your appointment with death that day on the river. Alban had been your friend, perhaps your closest, but neither had you confided in him.

These thoughts were suddenly and unpleasantly interrupted by another summons from the Master. I suppressed a groan when I heard his voice on the phone. Despite my affection and sympathy for him I was beginning to dread any contact with him, chance or otherwise.

'Thank you for coming, Alan,' he said, opening the door to the lodgings the moment I reached it. He must have been watching from the window. His stoop was now noticeably more pronounced than when we had seen your father together, and the strain in his features spoke of constant worry and sleepless nights. He handed me a glass of sherry he had already poured out. Yet again he chose whisky for himself, an even larger glass than before.

'It's awful, Alan,' he muttered, shaking his head. 'There's another one. A missing student, I mean.'

An image flashed through my mind. A body caught in the sluice gate of a water mill. Not you this time. Alban, his long, black hair floating in the water.

'This college?' I stammered. 'Another one of ours?'

Alban had known you. Alban had grieved for you. Alban had met me, entrusted me with a secret, had arranged to meet me again but had failed to turn up. It had to be him. It could not be a coincidence. I bit my lip, telling myself not to betray what I knew, however little that was.

'No. Dr Holmes just rang me from St Cuthbert's. He had heard about our tragedy. Obviously wondering if the same thing had happened there. One of his students didn't turn up for a tutorial, no explanation. His scout said he hadn't slept in his room for a week. No request for an exeat. Holmes had rung his parents in case there was a family crisis. But he hadn't been in touch with them, either. The parents asked him not to contact the police yet. Students sometimes just do wander off and either they come back or they don't. They're old enough. Not children any more. They can make their own choices. His mother said he was something of a free spirit, would sometimes go off hitchhiking in Europe at a moment's notice and they wouldn't know. Not until they got a phone call from some remote corner of Yugoslavia or something. Would have been nice if he'd had the decency to tell them this time, as well as us. But it does happen like that sometimes. Doesn't it?'

Name, please, for God's sake, what's his name?

'The name meant nothing to me. Or to you, I suppose. Knight. Alban Knight.'

I shrugged my shoulders, struggling desperately to maintain an air of calm reassurance. Yes, students do sometimes decide to call it a day and just disappear. Except that this time I knew better. Alban had been devastated by your suicide. He thought himself to be in danger, from whatever secret was in the envelope he had entrusted to my care, from someone he suspected was following him. There was surely some connection, at least in his mind, between your death and the threats he perceived. Now he too had disappeared. And the Master and his tutor did not know what I knew, that he had known you and had confided in me. I was not used to confidences. The burden of secrecy had already begun to weigh heavily on me. Now this. What would I tell the police if, or more likely when, they did get involved? I might have to disclose the contents of the envelope, perhaps incriminating myself in some dark affair and harming the reputation of the college, an offence which could lead to my summary dismissal. I dreaded the thought of another interview with the cynical inspector and his ambitious young sidekick. More to the point, what could I say to the Master now?

Fortunately I did not have to say anything. The phone rang. As he took the call I pointed to my watch to indicate I had another engagement. He smiled weakly and shrugged his shoulders, accepting that there was nothing useful I could say and that we both had other matters to attend to.

I had no other engagement. Back in my room, I took out the envelope and examined it from every angle, holding it to the light, feeling every inch of it for any telltale protrusions or outlines. It was brown, official-looking, the back reinforced by cardboard. No stamp. His name, forename and surname, was printed on it in black biro, with the name of his college underneath. In the top right-hand corner the same hand had written the instruction that it was to be delivered by hand to the addressee only. The weight and shape indicated the presence only of some flat sheets of paper.

I had no choice. I had to return the envelope to its place, unopened. And then, once again, I had to wait.

THIRTEEN

Life went on as it always does, nowhere more so than in Oxford. Beneath the surface ripple of chatter and laughter run the deep currents of seasons and terms and the cycles of essays, exams, cricket in the parks, slow punts on the Cherwell and the frantic surge of eights on the Isis, all hallowed by tradition and statute, custom and form. Our students come from all manner of places and from every walk of life, with every accent and style under the sun. Once here they are channelled into the pathways of study and recreation hollowed out by their predecessors over centuries. Some find it easy, or such is the appearance they give, others hard. But most emerge safely at the end, borne up by hopes and memories, ready for the future. Rarely does the river claim one of these expectant young lives for itself. Rarely does one simply disappear without trace. How often do both of these events occur in rapid succession, linked by mutual acquaintance?

My routines took over, my reactions to the questions of my students honed by years of experience into well-rehearsed responses which needed no conscious thought. At High Table dinner and Senior Common Room tea I was surrounded by the same marginally gossipy, rarely malicious small talk about colleagues, barely aware of the occasional word which crossed my lips. Nobody seemed to notice anything was amiss. Such is the power of social routine and for once I was grateful for it. When I was alone in my room I sat in my chair, neglecting my reading and my correspondence, waiting for darkness to creep across the quad and through the window and for sleep to claim me and find me hours later, still fully dressed in the same chair.

It was after one such long evening as I dozed, visited by rapidly interchanging images of you and Alban and snatches of your conversations, no words emerging clearly enough for me to grasp their meaning, that the knock came on the door.

It was loud and insistent. I shuddered, swore, realised where I was and that I had cramp in my legs, all in one moment. Then I looked at my watch and swore again. Midnight. Could it be Alban? But what would he be doing there at that time of night, and how had he managed to get into the college? I stumbled to the door and peered into the ink-black of the area at the base of the stone staircase. A figure stepped out of the shadows.

'Max? What are you doing here?'

'I'm sorry to disturb you this late, Mr Harris. He wants to see you, urgently. I've got to take you to see him.'

I gaped at him. He was dressed formally as usual, though he could not have been on duty that night. If he had been he would never have deserted his post at the lodge.

'Who, Max? Who are you talking about?'

'The young man who's asking after you. He's the one missing from St Cuthbert's.'

'Alban?'

'Yes, that's the one. We have to go now. I didn't want to leave him alone but he insisted I fetch you, even if I had to wake you. He's really scared, Mr Harris. We have to go now. I see you're still dressed. Let's go. I'll explain on the way.'

Gasping with fear and relief I stumbled out of the door, slamming it behind me, locking it only when he reminded me, and followed him through the silent quads into the car park.

I expected a mid-range saloon. I was not prepared for the noisy, draughty, wretchedly uncomfortable MG. Max offered no explanation for the incongruity. The most formal of us are entitled to a wild side, I thought. How might mine have manifested itself, if I had ever allowed it to emerge? Certainly not with a sports car, nor any sort of car. I crouched in the passenger seat, shivering, terrifyingly close to the floor, the vibrations surging through my body, draughts whistling around my ears. Max had closed the canvas roof but it left so many gaps he might as well not have bothered.

'I've got a little place out in Wytham,' he said, as if that were all the explanation needed for this crazy midnight adventure.

The car raced up the deserted Woodstock Road. Or so it seemed. But when I glanced at the dashboard I saw we were only doing just above fifty. The car's actual performance was nowhere near what its appearance and sound indicated. He spoke again, as if picking up my reluctance to address the question which was really on my mind, namely, what the hell were we doing there?

'Bit of a hobby of mine, Mr Harris. Old sports cars. They don't do much. Certainly not this one. All mouth and trousers, no real horsepower. Had this since I was barely out of nappies. I've rebuilt the engine twice. Sorry if it's a bit noisy.'

I tried without success to imagine him in oil-stained overalls bending over an open bonnet, spanner in hand.

At the Wolvercote roundabout he swung into a narrow country lane swathed in darkness. It wound through ghostly villages and over narrow bridges. Not for a second did he relax a speed which now seemed reckless, adjusting to the slow reaction of the steering wheel with the confidence of one who knew the car as well as his own body. Just before Wytham village he slammed on the brakes and wrenched the car into an unlit side road. The low-slung headlamps flashed on walls and hedges just before we had to hit them, though somehow we did not. He stopped before a one-storey cottage, a dim yellow light burning from a narrow, crooked window. I groaned with relief. He switched off the engine and helped me out of my side of the car. I was shaking.

'This is my little retreat,' he said, casually, as if it was his routine to drag dons there in the middle of the night without notice. 'He's in the front room. Light's still on.'

Alban was slumped in a huge armchair, dressed in a loose, faded dressing gown with a blanket over his knees. On a side table in front of him was a half-finished bowl of soup. He looked even paler and thinner than when I had last seen him. He glanced up, opened his mouth as if to speak, then looked down again.

'Sit down, Mr Harris,' said Max. 'I'll get you a little brandy. You look as if you could do with it.'

I sat down in an armchair opposite Alban. The room was long and narrow, the low ceiling supported by a heavy cross of sagging oak beams. In the grate between our chairs smouldered the remnants of an unseasonal wood fire. A folding dining table and two Windsor chairs stood near the door. The only other furniture was a wall-high bookcase behind Alban's chair, crammed with hardback books stacked at every angle. Porters, even head porters, are not usually well read, I thought. If he was truly familiar with even a fraction of those books there were a few tutors in college for whom he could have deputised at tutorials. Maybe even me.

Max brought in a bottle of brandy and three glasses and placed them on the table. He poured two glasses and offered them to us, standing between us and spreading out his arms to do so. I took mine gratefully. Alban shook his head. Max returned to the table, poured his glass and turned to us.

'I suppose I'd better explain,' said Max after a long pause, during which Alban's eyes flickered from mine to his and back again as if unsure where he was or who we were. 'I know this young man here was a friend of the other young gentleman, the one who passed away so tragically. Your student, Mr Harris. I saw him, this young man I mean, in the street the other day and recognised him. I was going to go up and have a quick chat, tell him how sorry I was, but then he got scared and seemed to think I was following him. Well, you can't blame him, can you? I knew who he was. Not by name then, but I knew he was a friend of your student. But he had no idea at all who I was. Head porter in another college, why should he know? Anyway, he slipped away and I thought no more about it. Until the other night, when I was checking on the other young man's room. As you know, Mr Harris, it's out of bounds. I wanted to be sure it was okay, that nobody had been in there. It's still locked, of course. I'm the only one with a key. I found this young man outside, sitting on the floor. In a hell of a state, weren't you?'

Max beamed an avuncular smile on Alban, who smiled back, weakly.

'He told me he needed to get inside the room,' Max continued. It seemed to have been agreed between them that he would do the talking. 'He told me he was sure there was something in there, something for him which the other young man, Simon, the one who… had left for him. He was your special friend, wasn't he?' He spoke the last words to Alban, who nodded. 'So I explained that there was nothing at all in the room. It had all been cleared out. Nothing could have been missed. Then he asked me why I was following him. I said I had only seen him by chance, once in college with his friend and the other day in the street. I had wanted to have a quick, friendly word. I hadn't meant to frighten him.'

Again he turned to Alban. 'You do understand that now, don't you?' Again the nod, barely perceptible. He turned back to me. 'He told me he was scared to go back to his college. Somebody had sent him something there, he said, something which had scared him. He didn't want to tell me any more and I didn't press him. That's still all I know. All right, I said. If you're scared to go back to your college, and there's nothing here for you in his room, certainly nothing for you to be gained from sitting outside it, then I can put you up at my place here for a few days. Nobody will know where you are. But just for a few days, mind. But I wouldn't let him come with me until he told me his name. He was reluctant at first. But I said we had to trust each other, and that had to start with names. I told him who I was, then a bit about me, how I came to be head porter. I could see he was starting to trust me. So here we are. He won't let me get a doctor. Says he's fine though you can see that he doesn't exactly look it. I've had the devil's own job just getting him to eat a little something.' Again he turned to his charge. 'I see you managed some of that soup. That's good.'

He nodded towards the half-empty bowl, smiling again. I was relieved. Alban could not have been in better hands.

'He needs help,' he continued. 'But up until this evening he wouldn't let me do anything for him. Got me to swear I wouldn't tell anybody where he is, not until he said so. I told him I had to contact his college about him. And someone needed to tell his parents. Nobody knows where he is. He'll fall behind with his studies. He needs some counselling, I'm sure. And maybe special arrangements for him to catch up, when he's ready. But still he wouldn't let me. Not until this evening. It was already quite late. Then suddenly and out of the blue he told me I had to fetch you and bring you here. I didn't want to disturb you at this hour but I was so relieved he wanted to talk to someone else. So I drove straight out to get you. I'm out of my depth, Mr Harris. I'm so pleased you're here.'

I took a sip of my brandy.

'Max is right, Alban,' I said, as gently as possible. 'You need help, and you can't stay here. Can I tell your tutor where you are?'

He shook his head, violently, leaning forward with an effort.

'Not yet. No, not yet.' His voice was thin, shaking, barely controlled. 'Have you seen them?'

'Seen what, Alban? I don't understand.'

His eyes opened a fraction wider. Surprise?

'You mean, you didn't open it?'

'No, of course not. I promised not to. I keep my promises.'

He slumped back into his chair.

'I want you to open it, Mr Harris. Tonight when you go back. Open it when you're on your own and don't tell anybody. Then I'll come and see you tomorrow.'

I glanced at Max, who nodded.

'That's fine,' said Max, addressing me. 'I'll drive him over to you.'

I leaned forward to Alban, who had shifted his body towards the fire and was staring into its depths. As I spoke, his eyes began to close.

'Listen, Alban, after we have spoken tomorrow, I'll see your tutor, if you agree, and your Master. We'll find somewhere for you to stay.'

He shook his head. 'I don't need the Warneford. I'm not mad.'

'I wasn't thinking of there, Alban. I'm sure you don't need to go to hospital. There are alternatives. Hostels. Where you will feel safe. There will be people to keep an eye on you. You can carry on with your studies. You can return to college when you feel ready. And your parents must be told you are safe.'

He had closed his eyes. I turned to Max. 'Better take me back now. I'm very grateful to you. This was over and above the line of duty.'

He stiffened and raised his chin as if back in the army, silently adopting the appropriate manner for one receiving praise from a senior officer. I imagined he had done so more than once. He stood up and raised the blanket up to Alban's chin. Alban was snoring quietly.

'He hasn't slept for nights, Mr Harris. It's because of you he's sleeping now. He's so relieved to see you. I can tell that. I have no idea what this is all about and I'm not one to pry. But I only want to know… will he be all right?'

'Yes, Max. It will be hard for him, maybe for a long time. But somehow I think he will be all right.'

FOURTEEN

I locked my door before settling down in my armchair to open the envelope. After a few minutes I re-inserted the contents and returned it to its hiding place. I turned off the light, went back to my chair and closed my eyes.

The silence and the dark were total, all-enveloping. Alone in a desert, or on an uninhabited island, I would have felt at least part of something, a world which was still there though I had no means of finding it again. But what surrounded me now was oblivion, a nothingness where a universe might once have been, drained of all time, energy and light.

Alban. My lips moved soundlessly to the syllables. What did he mean to me? He was not my student, not even of my college. I had no academic, no pastoral responsibility for him. He was young, innocent, helpless, reaching out to me for salvation. Yes, innocent, though some would not see the photographs I had just examined as innocent. What use was I to him, a middle-aged virgin don, unknown to life beyond a small circle in my brain? I would help him if I could, then he would move on and forget me. But I would never forget him. He had unknowingly torn open an old wound in me from which the blood would always flow. That, rather than the comfortable, amiable eccentricity of the life of an ageing bachelor was the destiny which now awaited me.

Spouse, sibling, lover, son, daughter, friend. Most of us find at least some of these in our lives at some point, even if we are not looking. I had somehow missed them all. Nothing had ever stirred within me of the excitement and sense of discovery and ecstasy and heartache which had obsessed others, which had told me they were alive but not told me how to join them in that venture.

So what was stirring now? Was it some form of belated adolescence, a beast lurking within of whose very existence I had been unaware? Lust? What did the word mean for one of my senses, atrophied from birth? I had known of it only as one of the deadly sins. The body had meant nothing to me, male or female, abstract or in the flesh. My early indoctrination had always seemed sufficient explanation of this central puzzle of life, even though I had never embraced the faith in which I had been brought up. The body means nothing in itself, I had been told. It houses the mind and the soul. The body ages and dies and the mind with it, sometimes before it. The soul lives on. The body is imperfect. The soul is perfect, unless we soil it with sin.

Now I knew they had lied to me. Now I had seen naked flesh, two young bodies, their very perfection a screaming rebuke to all those cold, life-denying edicts. But that was not all I had seen, not by any means. I had seen life, his and yours, all the reaching out and the touching and the smiling and the trust of it. I had seen love.

Was that my wound? Love does not need to be returned or even recognised. It can just be given. Without warning, someone had just come into my life whom I had just as suddenly decided to love, chastely, selflessly, without mutuality, without even a declaration, but with a total abandonment of heart. That could have been my salvation, my hope for a redemption I had never expected to find. Briefly, briefly beyond measure, the hope had flickered in my breast before I realised it had to die, aborted before it had drawn a single breath, because it could never be other than an insult to its object. Now I knew exactly how insulting. There, in those images, was the final rejection, the end of a way and a truth and a life I had barely begun to make out through the mist. The intended object of my selfless love had loved already, not selflessly, not chastely, but mutually and with passionate declaration. His lover had gone, but that love still occupied his whole being. My sort of love was as momentary and invisible as the flash of a sub-atomic particle. If he had been granted the means to see it, he would have treated it with the contempt it deserved.

No, loneliness was my wound, as it had been all along, now infinitely worse for what I had just seen.

FIFTEEN

I knew it was Max at the door. Three firm, decisive knocks, then the polite wait for me to respond. He looked round, then stood back, allowing Alban to enter. As Alban did so, Max let a protective hand fall on his shoulder before withdrawing it and himself, silently telling us that he was bowing out, passing his charge from his care to mine.

I gestured for Alban to sit in your chair. He did so clumsily, as if this most everyday movement of an undergraduate in a tutor's room was already a stranger to his memory. He looked up at me, dark rims around his eyes, the eyes themselves red and swollen from crying and lack of sleep. I sat in my usual chair and leaned forward.

'Are you all right? Has Max looked after you well?'

He nodded, then looked away.

'The other day, in the chapel, you said you thought you were being followed. You know now that it was only Max and that he was concerned for you. Is that right? You've not noticed anybody else?'

He shook his head. I rose and looked out of the large bay window which gave on to the quad. I could see the entrance to the porters' lodge. I would be able to see anyone who had come through the lodge and was lurking near my staircase. But not someone who might be listening directly outside. I opened my door, looked out, then came back in.

'Nobody there,' I said, trying to sound as reassuring as I could. I returned to my chair.

'So, Alban, tell me about the photographs.'

He looked down, his hand hovering in front of his mouth.

'No, I don't mean about what they show,' I added, hastily. 'I'm not here to judge that. You must realise that or you would never have given them to me. I mean how you came to have them.'

What was there to judge? Two young people sitting on a park bench, holding hands, gazing into each other's eyes. The same couple walking side by side, engaged in private conversation. The same couple standing together, naked, by the bank of the river. It was a well-known if secluded spot, called Parson's Pleasure, mostly frequented by male dons with a penchant for nude bathing. Everybody knew about it. It was visible from the river as you punted past. For ladies who wished to avoid embarrassment there was a rollerway over which punts could be pulled to bypass that stretch of the river. Yet some would judge, if only because the couple were two young men, about nineteen.

He sat still, silent, shifting position slightly in the chair, as if in that awkward moment between his finishing the reading of an essay and my starting to comment. I had to lead him on, in the hope that at some point he would feel safe enough to open up.

'All right,' I said. 'I'll talk. Just tell me if I get something wrong. Did you know they were being taken? I presume not.

I'll also presume that you do not know who took them. You received them anonymously. Simon also received copies.'

I looked at him carefully as I spoke, watching for his reactions. With those last words, he shook his head violently.

'No. I mean, yes. Or rather, I don't know.'

His voice croaked. His nose was running. He took out a tissue and wiped it.

'Alban, are you all right to continue with this? Do you want to rest? You can lie down here. At the back. Nobody will disturb you. Do you need anything to drink, or eat? Max said you weren't eating. We can get you through all this somehow, but you mustn't let yourself get ill.'

'No, I'm fine.'

He raised his head, stiffened his body and looked me in the eye for the first time since he had entered the room. I rose, went to my private space and poured two tumblers of water. He accepted his hesitantly, as if unsure what it was, then sipped it slowly. I waited.

'I got them in that envelope,' he said, almost whispering. 'A couple of days after Simon's death. Someone had given it to the porter to give to me by hand. I have no idea if Simon had seen them as well. You didn't find anything like them in his things, did you?'

'No. I went through everything. Was that why you wanted to look inside his room? When Max found you?'

'No. I was wondering about something else. You told me he didn't leave a note. I couldn't believe that. I couldn't believe that he would just go and say nothing. Maybe he wouldn't want to leave a note for the police or his parents. But surely he had left something for me. He just wouldn't do that. Go away like that without telling me why. Or even saying goodbye. Go away forever. I searched everywhere. My own room, in case he had slipped in while I wasn't there. I looked in places where we had been together. Nothing. Then I went up to his room but it was locked. I waited there, God knows what for.'

'The room was empty, Alban, completely cleared out. You must believe that.'

He nodded and buried his face in his hands. I waited. There were practicalities to be discussed but I had to choose my moment. It came a few minutes later, when at last he looked up again. He took out another tissue, this time drying his eyes.

'You can stay here and rest for a few hours,' I said. 'Maybe even overnight, just once.' It was a dangerous suggestion, given that gossip was a favourite donnish pastime. No rumours had to my knowledge ever circulated about me, so one time was surely safe. More than once was another matter. 'But you really should go back to your college. See the college doctor and decide if you need anything. I can ring your tutor when I know you are on the way. Or I can go with you.'

He rose slowly from his chair, shaking his head.

'I'll go back now. I can manage on my own. I'll see the college nurse tomorrow. She's on duty in the morning. Thank you for everything.'

At the door he turned back. 'You know you suggested I might come to you for a tute. Just a pretend.'

'Yes, I remember.'

'Could we still do that?'

'Of course. Let me know when you can come. Remind me. What was your essay on?'

'The Peterloo Massacre.'

'I'll look forward to learning about it.'

SIXTEEN

O f course it was just a pretend, to use the words he had retrieved from his childhood games. But he entered exactly as if for a tutorial, clutching a folder of papers. His gown was slightly askew, thrown on in the haste of nervous preparation. He looked suitably anxious. I waved him once again to your chair and sat down opposite. He ruffled through the folder, then glanced up, nervously.

'I forgot to ask about the envelope last time, Mr Harris. Is it—'

'Don't worry, Alban. Safely stowed, same place as before. One key and I always have it on me.'

He grinned, to my surprise. In just a week he had recovered much of his natural poise and there was just a little colour in his cheeks. I imagined his friends had with the spontaneous kindness of youth, a kindness that has not yet learned to count the cost and hold back, done all in their power to cheer him up.

'"Safely stowed", Mr Harris? I suppose a tute on *Hamlet* would do as well as any. Better for me than *Beowulf*.'

I felt a pang of envy for the light undergraduate banter in which he was still able to indulge.

'*Hamlet* is off for me as well, I'm afraid. Did you want to talk a bit more about the photographs? Are you ready for that? There are some serious questions we need to consider.'

'Okay.'

'We don't know if Simon got copies as well. If he did, there's no sign of them. But what we do know is that someone went to the trouble of watching you and taking them, all without either of you having a clue it was happening. If you think he was being blackmailed you should take them to the police, or let me do it. Especially if you think you are going to be blackmailed in your turn. Though as yet nobody has contacted you, have they?'

'No, they haven't. Letting me stew, maybe. I understand what you are saying. Blackmail is against the law. But so is that. I mean, what we were, what we did. Those photos could have destroyed both of us. They could still destroy me. If they have other copies and send them to the Master of my college, or to the proctors, I could be sent down.'

I had thought of that and had my response ready.

'No, I don't believe that. There's no evidence there of any misconduct on college or university premises. I would speak up for you, if it came to anything serious like that. I owe that to him. And to you, for taking me into your confidence. As for the police, they surely wouldn't do anything against you, especially if you helped them find a blackmailer. In any case, things are changing. I don't know much about this sort of thing. But I know the law has changed.'

'Not for us. Not for anyone under twenty-one. Not yet.'

'Did you have any idea at all that anyone might be watching you?'

'None at all. I've been thinking it over. Perhaps they sent him copies and got in touch with him. He must have thought they were the only ones. Somehow he thought his death would get us both off the hook. I can't imagine what they wanted or why he felt that killing himself was the only way out. It can't have been for money. He didn't have money. Neither do I. Look, you must promise not to tell the police anything. Please.'

'All right, no police. But you will tell me if you are contacted? You will promise me that? You must trust me. Simon didn't and I blame myself for that. I was too distant from him.'

'But he and I weren't distant. And I thought he would have trusted me with his life. I would have trusted him with mine. Even if this isn't about blackmail, even if nobody contacts me, I still need your help. I need to know exactly why and how he died, why he chose to face whatever he thought the danger was on his own. And all that stuff you told me, about the whisky and the pills. I just don't get that. It wasn't him. To be planning it all like that when I'm so sure he couldn't have been or I would have known. Will you help me?'

He looked up. A tear trembled on his lower eyelid. It trickled slowly down his cheek. Another followed. That was all. He blinked and brushed away the traces.

'I'll do all I can,' I said. 'But first you must help me. Tell me all you know about him. Start with when and how you met.'

'Tomorrow. Let's take a punt out.'

He was far more skilled at punting than I would ever have been. I was content to sit back and direct him to the bend in the river which was our destination. He steered into the bank. I jumped out and moored the punt to a protruding branch. I climbed back in and opened the packed lunch I had brought.

'Was this the actual spot?' he asked, munching with surprising appetite on a cheese sandwich.

'Near enough. This is where his punt was found. The whisky and pill bottles were inside.'

'So let's imagine the scene.' There was a steely look in his eyes, the previous day's tears forgotten.

'Are you sure you're up to this, Alban?'

'Yes. I have to do it. So, he takes the punt out on his own, after somehow getting hold of the whisky and pills without anybody noticing. Nobody has the slightest clue what he intends, not me, not you. He ties up here, drinks nearly all the whisky, takes all the pills. Enough to kill him. Yes?'

'Yes.'

'But he was not dead when he entered the water.'

'That's right, according to the coroner. Drowning was the immediate cause.'

'So why did he go into the water? Why not just lie down here and pass away peacefully?'

'Maybe he had a last-minute change of mind. He felt himself losing consciousness. He managed to roll over into the water in an attempt to shock himself awake, so he could vomit up what he had swallowed. It didn't work.'

He grunted. 'Could be. Another thing. There are undergraduate suicides every year here. I mean, in Oxford.'

'Tragically, yes.'

'How many are on the river?'

'None I've ever heard of. Most take place in the students' own rooms.'

'Methods?'

'God, I'm no expert. Some hang themselves. Some take pills. The ones who take pills are usually making a cry for help rather than a serious attempt. Anything involving blood, like wrist-slitting, is more rare. All that is just my impression, from anecdotes.'

'So this one could be unique.'

'It could well be. But the intention seems clear enough. He came here to die. We know about the whisky and the pills. They were for one purpose only.'

'And we know about the photographs. They're all connected.'

'Okay. Let's think about the photographs. Someone had sent him copies, let's presume. No, let's go back a stage. Someone knew about you and followed you, secretly. Took the pictures without your knowledge. That takes some doing. A long-distance lens. Expensive camera. Know anyone with a camera like that?'

'No. I have a cheap Kodak Instamatic. There are quite a few of those around. But this was a professional job, wouldn't you say? Not just the camera. Following us without being spotted.'

'When were they taken? All on the same day, or over a period? Do you remember?'

'That's another curious thing. They are spread over some weeks. He was on our trail all that time and we never knew.'

'So either a professional doing a job, or a highly motivated and expert amateur. And if a professional, who was paying him and why? We have to focus on what was special about the two of you. I'm sorry but there is no getting away from this. It has to be about the nature of your relationship.'

He laughed. 'Because we were queers. But it surely can't be blackmail, if you think about it. As I said, neither of us had money.'

I remembered what I had seen of your bank statement. A payment to your brother. A few thousand. Bigger money than most undergraduates would ever dream of. But small change for a blackmailer. They deal in tens of thousands, minimum. What would it cost to employ someone to do that spying job? A few thousand at least.

'So, if it's not for blackmail,' he continued, 'why send copies of the photographs to me after his death?'

'A warning?'

'To do what?'

'Nothing. That's the point. To keep quiet about your relationship.'

'Which I would anyway. You said I wouldn't be sent down, but things would be different if they found their way into the press.' With a sudden movement he put his hand to his mouth.

'Alban, what is it?'

'Maybe that's it. We talked about it several times. He wanted to be open about us. He said people should know. Family, friends. You as well, maybe. He was tired of being secretive, feeling dirty. He said we had nothing to be ashamed about. I told him I had never felt ashamed and never would. But I still thought we should be careful. He might have told somebody, without my knowing, someone who decided to betray his confidence. Maybe he realised then what he had done. He had put both of us in danger of exposure. So somehow he thought his death would put the genie back in the bottle. But who would he have told?'

'There is another possibility. He told nobody. Let's say a photographer from a newspaper has been sniffing around, trying to get dirt on undergraduate goings-on. I mean there is a lot more sexual freedom these days, isn't there? Even I've noticed that. He spotted you two, that time in the park, holding hands. Followed you. He knew about Parson's Pleasure. Seeing you there gave him a chance for something really juicy. He contacted Simon. Promised to destroy the pictures if...'

'If what? If Simon gave him an even juicier story? A student who kills himself because he can't bear the thought of what would happen when the story hits the headlines? But I told you. He wanted it all out in the open. Not in the press, of course. But not secret any more.'

'But there's a difference, isn't there? Between an understanding among family and friends about the nature of your love and sensational revelations in the press with pictures taken out of context? That would have been the opposite of what he wanted. That would have brought it all on both of you, on your families, on the college and the university, all the shame and disgrace he was trying to dispel.'

He pondered for a few moments, a half-eaten apple in his hand. At last he discarded it into the river.

'So maybe it's a journalist who's after us,' he said. 'From the gutter press, I believe they call it. And the fact that I have the photos now suggests the story may still be live. He'll contact me for my angle in his own time.'

'Or he could be freelance and looking for someone to buy his story. In which case it may well come to nothing. Who else knew about the two of you? As far as you know.'

'I told nobody. I was going to tell my family after he had told his. He was more worried about his. Mine are pretty easy-going. Very liberal. They think the age of consent should be sixteen now. They probably suspect I'm that way inclined. His parents are more strait-laced. He never said anything about what his brother might think. I doubt if he'd care. He's obsessed with his business.'

'That was my impression too. What about Simon's religious beliefs? I met the priest at the funeral. He told me Simon was a devout Catholic.'

'You think it might be a guilt thing, suddenly coming back to haunt him? No. He wasn't religious any more. He told me he dropped all that in his first term.'

'All right, not his guilt. But what about someone who thought he should feel guilty. A fanatic. A Bible-thumper.

Someone who thinks we're all going to hell in a handcart, and the law should never have been changed. They got hold of the photographs, or learned about you two and commissioned them. Then they contacted Simon, telling him what they had on him, showing him copies of the evidence. He was given certain promises, assurances, in return for... what? His death to destroy the photographs and to spare you. He would tell you nothing, certainly not leave you a note. Except, of course, that they weren't all destroyed. You got copies and there may well be others in existence. But maybe the deal was your life for his. One death is enough. The debt is paid. You got copies so you know they know. So you know they have the power to destroy you. But they won't if you keep quiet. And avoid any such liaisons in the future. But the fact remains that nobody has contacted you other than to leave the photographs. And if that is the way it stays then we will never know. So let's put all that to one side for now. I want to know more about the two of you. How did you first meet?'

Teach me, Alban. I am the tutor who knows nothing. Teach me what I never knew. Teach me about love.

SEVENTEEN

'It was the music. That's how we met. I was taking a shortcut through your college, from St Giles to Parks Road. I passed beneath the window of the music room. It was a warm day so the window was open. He was playing the piano. Liszt. The first concerto, second movement. The opening melody. Sad and beautiful, all at once. A song from heaven. I had no idea who it was, of course. Could have been anybody.

'It wasn't easy to play. That was really why I stopped to listen. He was having some difficulties with one passage. Going over it several times. Trying to get to the essence of it. I suspected it wasn't a music student or anybody like that. They'd have been doing something much flashier. Showing off their technique. This was an amateur, in the best sense of the word. I didn't want to disturb whoever it was. I went inside and listened at the door. He stopped and I heard the piano lid close. That was when I went in. I had planned things to say, about how beautiful and moving it was, what a lovely touch he had. Or she. As I said, it could have been anybody. When I saw him I was tongue-tied. Just speechless.

'That had never happened to me before. It wasn't my first relationship. There was somebody at school I was close to. It was only a bit physical. Some kissing and cuddling. But it was easy and natural between us from the start. We were always able to talk, about our school subjects, sports, our teachers, politics, life and the universe, the awful school grub. Just talk for hours and chat and laugh. With Simon it was always going to be different. Awkward. I think I was the first to speak. I mumbled something about being sorry to have disturbed him. That was stupid because it was obvious he had finished his session so I wasn't disturbing him. He thought I was the next person due in the room, that I had booked the next hour for my own practice. I followed him out, trying to explain that I wasn't there to play, that I couldn't play anything, that I had heard him from outside and wanted to… well, I couldn't say what. Not at that time.

'So we walked around the quad and the gardens, still without saying much. I had forgotten that I was on my way back to my college. He had forgotten whatever it was he was going to do next. There was a spell surrounding us as we walked, and each of us was terrified of breaking it by saying the wrong thing or even saying anything at all. In the end we sat down on a bench in the gardens and I managed to tell him what I had loved about the music and the way he played it. I was apologising even though I hadn't actually disturbed him. I mean, I could have just listened and walked on. But I couldn't. So I told him and the spell didn't break. I remembered I had an essay to finish by five o'clock. I told him my name and what college I was at and what my room number was and invited him for tea the following afternoon. Still the spell did not break. All that tedious reality about the details of arranging when and where to meet again and the spell did not break. He was staring after me when I got up to leave. I could sense it. I turned round and smiled and he was smiling. That was when we knew this was different. The spell would never break, not unless someone or something broke it for us.

'Well, I finished my essay after a fashion. It was my worst by far. Gamma query minus. I had to write it again. It wasn't much better the second time. I think my tutor suspected I had fallen in love. Simon and I met for tea the next afternoon and we chatted a bit. It was funny. Our second meeting was far more of a strain than the first. We often didn't finish our sentences. We'd start to talk about our subjects or our home lives and just dry up. Then without saying anything I got up and locked the door. Slowly, so he could object if he wanted to. But he seemed to understand. Then I drew the curtains. We kissed and held each other and got into bed together.

'It was such a relief not to have to find any more words. Not until afterwards. Then we didn't need words. Just more tea. He made it. I watched him from the bed, moving around my room as if he had always been part of it. He was at home, full of ease, casual, naked, his body moving into and out of the shadows cast by the light through the curtain. It was as if the light and the shadows and his movements were sculpting his body afresh every few seconds, finding new aspects of beauty and grace. I just lay there and watched and wondered. There was no need to talk then. There was no past and no future, just the present. And the present moves from moment to moment and no words can interrupt it.

'We did talk, of course. Later on that day. And on other days. When there was space and time. And when there wasn't it didn't matter. Until the day he told me. When he said those words. I had started the relationship but he was the one who said the words. Not theatrically, or melodramatically. Just casually, one day as we walked through the Parks. We were alone. Or I was sure we were. I can't be sure now, of course.

But this was some time ago. Long before the earliest of those photos. He just came out with it. "I love you." Of course, I said that I loved him too. It wasn't needed. It was understood. I knew and he knew. But once we had said it we knew there was no going back.

'We knew what might lie ahead. Well, no might about it. We would face it. Prejudice, hatred, contempt, just for being who we were. But one thing I never thought we would face would be one of us dying. Not so soon. Not within just a few months.'

EIGHTEEN

I love you.

    While I listened to him, I was thinking of you. His voice flowed softly, melodious with love and grief, like the music he had heard you play. If only I had a memory of your playing which I could have shared with the man you loved. When he came to that last part, about hearing and speaking those three words, it seemed to ease his heartache even as he recounted it.

My own memories were stirring. I had never spoken those words but now they sounded once again in my ears. Yes, someone had once said them to me, many years before. It is time to tell you about Father Anselm.

He always had a special smile for me. Why me? Perhaps it was because we had not met in the expected way, at my boarding school, but on the train taking us both there for the first time. There were just the two of us in the enclosed compartment. Intimacy of some sort was compulsory.

'Where are you off to, young man?'

That smile. I did not know then that it was special, just for me.

'Fidelis College, Father.'

Then the laugh, deep and resonant, frightening. What was it for? Where had it come from? How was I supposed to react? I could not laugh back. I had never learned. I had read about laughter but never heard it. Nobody in our house ever laughed. At my first school there would often be titters and giggles amid the surrounding chatter in the playground and in the classroom before the arrival of the teacher, about secrets into which I would never be let and would never have understood anyway. They came from the mouth, out of the sides and corners, from the same place as whispers and sneers. This was different. This came from within, from somewhere deep inside that huge belly and cavernous chest.

'Small world. That's where I'm going.'

We talked, in a way I knew would be impossible once we were at the school, master and twelve-year-old pupil, no longer fellow travellers on a train. He was red-faced, with deep black eyes that frightened me as much as the voice, until that smile. So we talked. About music (he knew far more than I ever would), art, literature, language. Here, already, he struck a chord and he knew it.

The school was a former stately home deep in the stark countryside of Lancashire, miles from the nearest town. All of us were boarders. Some had been such from the start and would have been under any circumstances. They were relaxed and confident, the comfortable security of their past and present pointing to a successful future in which they would lead the rebuilding of the shattered nation, once victory had come. The rest of us were only there because of the war, easily distinguishable by our drab uniforms, the absence of letters or gifts from home, our shy, nervous mannerisms. We were ripe for bullying from our more privileged peers, and that was what I expected. But to my surprise it never happened. We shared privations in our daily lives to which I was accustomed and which they seemed to find amusingly novel, the cold and the draughts, the hard narrow beds in the dormitories, the snoring of those pupils who were cursed with bronchitis, the solid and monotonous food. Despite our isolation it seemed that we were all aware of massive, violent changes in the wider world which made arbitrary differences between us seem unimportant. We applied ourselves with deadly seriousness to our studies, knowing there was a huge task ahead for all, once we had left those protecting walls (yes, it was yet another place in my life dominated by walls). We were wise and mature beyond our years.

Father Anselm paid me particular attention, helping me with my essays, giving me extra lessons, letting me have books on loan and forgetting to ask for them back. Always that smile when we passed in the corridor or glimpsed each other in the playground. I now knew it was reserved for me. I never saw it focus on anyone else.

In our private lessons he would lean close to check what I was writing, enough for me to feel his warmth and smell the tobacco on his breath. Sometimes he would place his hand on my shoulder, always gently. On one of those occasions, several weeks after our first meeting, he bent down and whispered the three words. Low but unmistakable. That was all. It was a freely offered gift, never to be repeated, by him or anyone else. He demanded nothing in return.

Was that why in later life I never offered love or sought it for myself, not until the moment I had decided to offer Alban what I understood to be the trappings of love, the care and attention and concern, everything but that essence which can come only from declaration, from saying and hearing those words? I had no understanding of that essence, not until I heard Alban describe it to me that day on the river. Perhaps Father Anselm had given me something too precious and fragile to risk breaking it. Even to admit to myself the possibility of closeness with anybody would break it as surely as an egg would break if I dropped it on a stone floor. It was that momentary gift of love, unsought, undeserved, untarnishable by time and the world because outside of both, which I so desperately wanted to shelter and protect. I knew I would never know its purity, its sheer unadulterated divinity, again.

Maybe that is the truth of it. Or maybe I am deceiving myself and not for the first time. Maybe my fear is not of losing something precious, but of being seen and known for what I really am, whatever that may be. I do not know, but I am sure of one thing. Though not yet twenty, Alban had lived a life far fuller and more intense and truthful and human than any I would ever now have a chance to live. And so had you.

Because you had both dared to reach out and touch. But for me, touch had been sullied by the one person who had declared love for me. I found this out only after his sudden and unexpected departure, from fellow pupils with far more alertness to the spreading word than I. They suspected nothing about his special feelings for me. But they knew why he had gone. In the showers at the gym and games field, in the privacy of his study, Father Anselm had laid intimately touching hands on boys for whom he felt no love. Me, whom he loved, he never touched, not like that. Word finally reached the Head and a hasty transfer was arranged. So for me, love and touch stood at opposite poles. I never knew, until you and Alban taught me, how they could complete each other and become as one.

I'd like to tell you another story about my childhood, another secret, if you can bear it. But you have patience enough. You had it while you were alive. I knew that. So did your priest. He mentioned it at your funeral service.

I used to play. Yes, it's true. If I had had even a fraction of your talent or your application, it might have been me in that room or one like it, years before Alban heard you, struggling to realise the sublime through my fingers and the hardness of the keys, not suspecting that I was reaching out to another's soul.

There was a tinny upright piano in the house, tucked away in the front room. The yellow ivory keys were worn and the pedals squeaked. The lettering intended to identify the maker had flaked away. Someone had once played it, over many years, whether bringing it to life or battering it into submission I could not know. One of the aunts in her youth, perhaps. Though it never occurred to me that any of them had ever had a youth. Nobody in the house played it now. It had not been tuned for decades. There was no sheet music in the moth-eaten piano stool or in any of the cupboards. One day, when I was about eight, my mother discovered me using one clumsy finger to pick out a tune I had heard on the radio. It was a poor approximation, but enough for her to decide I had something which called for development and discipline. I was clearly in need of both, my schoolwork being then distinctly unimpressive.

The next day I was sent to the local piano teacher. She lived in the next street so I could make my own way there. I stood outside her door for what seemed like hours, shaking with fright. I did not dare to knock for fear of the dragon which might lurk behind that door. Even less did I dare to go home and tell my mother I had lost my nerve. Miss Penhaligon, for that was her name, must have seen me from her window.

She opened the door and smiled. To me she seemed infinitely old. She was perhaps sixty, with silver hair tied in a bun and a stoop. She ushered me into her front room, where stood a baby grand piano, an instrument far more magnificent than any I had seen or imagined could exist.

The lessons were not a success, to put it mildly. We would spend the first few minutes working on my scales, for which I never retained a memory of what I had slowly and painfully learned from the previous lesson. Then we would try out a simple piece, though never simple enough for me. Then in the last ten minutes she would play for me. I sat and listened in wonder while she conjured magic spirits out of the wood and metal of the monstrous instrument which refused to yield anything to me but a dead, harsh noise. She played pieces by Bach, Mozart and Mendelssohn, though she never told me what they were and I only identified them much later in life, when a performance on the radio triggered a memory.

Miss Penhaligon had a sister. She looked to me every bit as ancient, though I later learned she was a few years younger, with the same hair done in the same way. Sometimes it was the sister who answered the door and told me she would be giving me my lesson that day. It would take me a few moments to realise it was she and not my usual teacher. The sister also performed at the end of my lessons, though she was a singer rather than a pianist. However, she was competent enough to be able to accompany herself in arias by Handel and songs by Schubert.

Miss Penhaligon and her sister were devoted to each other. One day I arrived for my lesson to be told by a tearful Miss Penhaligon that her sister had died suddenly from a heart attack. I did not understand what a heart attack was, but I had heard enough about death to know that her sister had gone and would not return. I sat down at the piano but never touched it that day. Speaking no longer in the rich, deep tones which the authority of her knowledge and her teacher's calling conferred on her but in the broken tones of personal grief, she told me of her sister's life in music and her career as a singer. This is one of the stories she told me. I remember it still. I have never passed it on to anyone before, but now I pass it on to you.

'My sister was singing at the Philharmonic once, about ten years ago,' she told me, 'with the orchestra, under Sir Adrian Boult. Handel's *Largo*. At the rehearsal the orchestra started off with the introduction. She knew straight away something was wrong. It was a tone too high for her. Not what she was used to. He knew right away there was a problem so he stopped. "What is it?" he asked her. "You're playing in G and I'm used to the key of F," she stammered. She was terrified of what he might do. He was already famous and distinguished. Her career was long past its peak. He would surely throw her out and get in someone else. And what would the orchestra be thinking? They had the music there on the stands. In the key of G. All the different editions for the different instruments, all in the wrong key. They could not possibly get ones in a different key just for her. The performance was that night. It was her big chance to show she still had it in her. Why hadn't she said nothing and tried it in the higher key? What, and risk making an even bigger fool of herself by cracking on the high notes? She just wanted the earth to swallow her up. But he was smiling. He turned to the orchestra. His voice was so kind and gentle, but full of authority. I met him myself, after the performance, so I can vouch for that. He was a gentleman. "Ladies and gentlemen, in the key of F, please." They played it. Just like that. All of them. Transposing the music at sight. Just for her. She was nearly in tears. So was I when she told me about it.'

A few weeks later she too had passed away. Like her sister she had devoted her life to music. But it had not been enough to keep her alive after she was left alone. How could it be? I imagined them together in heaven, Miss Penhaligon accompanying her sister's singing, with a choir of angels adding a divine descant.

I was never sent to another teacher and I never touched the piano again. I sometimes wonder if my mother realised how little actual learning had taken place during the lessons for which she had paid.

NINETEEN

We sat together in the punt quietly after he had stopped speaking. He trailed a hand in the water, letting it flow across and beneath, like time. He was offering me a rare privilege. He was inviting me into his world, however brief and temporary the experience would be, to let me see and feel it the way he did.

How soon we forget how to deal with time. Only the young understand. They know that it moves at different paces, like the variegated depths of the currents beneath his fingers. It is fast and threatening when the dreaded tutorial deadline looms and the typewriter clatters. In the tutorial itself it moves slowly, taking the long minutes needed to absorb new ideas and fresh discoveries. At dinner in hall it is once again fast but in its own way. Ears need to be alert to several conversations at once, always ready to cut in with a joke or a jibe or a clever remark or just to listen and pick up something to be turned over in the mind at a quieter hour. Time is slow in the afternoons, during walks in the parks or while lingering on a bench, as thoughts gather and join up into arguments, or impressions are simply allowed at their own pace to penetrate the awareness within. In the pub with friends, relaxing after a tutorial and the elation of an essay well received or the despondency of one whose flaws have been mercilessly exposed, time is different again, as casual and ludicrous thoughts float to the surface. Solutions to the problems of the world, a little kindly gossip, an anecdote about the behaviour of a tutor, maybe even a little affectionate imitation of a mannerism, all permitted in the geniality of company and the knowledge that with the freedom provided by a pint or two of cheap beer no judgement will be passed, that the next day all will be forgotten except the smiles and the laughter, no folly, not even the worst of jokes from childhood, recalled or condemned.

So it is for the young. So it was for me, in my first few weeks as an undergraduate. Then I changed, started to become what I am now.

No, that is wrong. Why is it so hard for me to be honest? I was always what I am now. What changed was my growing realisation of that fact. I had been there in the pub with those friends, or so I thought them to be at the time. But I had not taken part in the laughter, the jokes, the anecdotes. Laughter was still a stranger to me. I could listen and perhaps force a little smile. It was as if I were at the theatre, in the audience rather than on the stage. I had nothing to offer the others and soon they realised that. So they moved on. They found girls. They sought out the company of male friends who had much more to offer than I. Like what? Wit, originality, even crudeness at times, a readiness to share the ebb and flow of their sexual adventures, to display vulnerability, to allow themselves to be laughed at as well as admired. I let them go. I did not fight to keep them. What choice did I have? Why should they waste their precious time with one with so little to give? I felt a darkness building up within me. I spent more and more time alone, in my room or out walking. My time became one-dimensional, crawling wearily from second to second. I lived in a brown fog through which I could see nothing, past, present or to come. Terms, seasons, fashions, all came and went and all wore the same dull garb.

It lifted at last, in a way. But by then I was truly on my own. I had fallen behind badly with my work. I picked it up again with a frenzy. It became my whole life. After finals my fellow students celebrated with champagne outside the Examination Schools. Even if I had been with them they would scarcely have recognised me. I looked ten years older than they did, than I had expected to look when I had started my undergraduate life with them.

I packed my bags and returned to my aunt, the one who had seen me off at the station to boarding school. She had assumed my grandmother's place in the house and her custom of sitting for hours in silence, her shoulders hunched in the same way. She wore identical clothes to hers. Perhaps she had taken over the selfsame ones. There were now only the two of us in the house. All the furniture from the years when the house had been full remained in place. Sheets had been thrown over it all, other than in the dining room, kitchen and the two bedrooms still in use. Dust gathered in heaps. Grime patterned the windows. The accumulated flies of years clung to the twisted strips of adhesive paper hanging from the ceilings.

My aunt accepted my presence but never asked about my plans. I was recalled to Oxford a month after finals for a viva examination, so they could decide if my borderline first-second result could be confirmed as a first. It was. Nothing stirred within me when I got the news. I did not tell my aunt. She would not have understood what it meant. There was nobody else to tell. A few weeks later I was invited back to do a postgraduate course, then offered a junior fellowship. Now I could live permanently in Oxford. At some point in the years that followed my aunt must have died, but I was never told. Who owns the house now or who lives there, God knows.

For me now, time is a cramped, hurried thing, too cluttered with paperwork and irksome duties and the endless rehearsal of knowledge long since gone stale. It brings no new insights, no new moments of self-reinvention, only the sense that a life not yet lived is itself running out of time. I have lived through the late 1960s, or rather watched them through a frosted window. Fashion, pop music, dope, psychedelia, free love, all been and gone without our even noticing each other.

There is a future, but it belongs to my students. Yes, they can be clumsy, inarticulate, foolish, maddening. That is the other side of the coin which is their youth. On this side is their beauty, their energy, their optimism, their belief that whatever they may do or get wrong in the now there will always be another chance. They reject the present their elders made and cannot wait to make their own.

You will notice that I speak of them and not of you. You never had the chance to join in making that future. It was so easy for me to think that like the others you would succeed because of all you shared with them, or appeared to share. If you were quieter, less outspoken than others, that was only to be expected. You had your own way to follow and you would surely reach your own destination in the end. So I did not reach out to share with you, and I now ask your forgiveness for that sin of omission. Because I know there was something we shared. A darkness invisible.

I shivered. A cool breeze drifted across the misty water. Gloom was beginning to shroud the trees. How much time had elapsed? Surely the punt was long overdue. Alban noticed my discomfort and clambered to his feet, the punt rocking slightly.

As he guided us back with steady, well-controlled strokes of the pole I gathered my thoughts, only now returning to the present and to the matter we had gone there to discuss.

'Maybe we'll never know exactly why he died,' I said, feeling it behoved me as his senior to sum up, however unqualified I felt to do so. 'The photographs obviously have something to do with it. Try to forgive him for not understanding the grief he would cause you. I'm sure he only wanted to protect you, from something he could barely understand himself. So all you can do now is respect that. Do what he would have wanted. Get on with your life. Do your work, get your degree, have whatever career you choose. Let's hope this business with the photographs blows over. I'll destroy them if you want.'

I wasn't sure he had heard me. He replied only after several more energetic pushes deep into the riverbed. The river was narrow at that point. He needed to concentrate on using the trailing end of the pole to steer after each push.

'Yes, you're right,' he said at last. 'That would be best. If someone wants to use them against me they'll have other copies. But surely I would have heard by now.'

'And keep in touch. If you ever have the slightest suspicion that anyone is following you, or if anyone does contact you about the photographs, you will tell me, won't you? Turn up as if for a tute, like you did yesterday. Nobody's to know you're not one of my students. All right?'

Please come, Alban, for whatever reason or none. Come and shine a light into my darkening days.

I took them out of the cupboard to look at them one last time, the youthful eyes so open to the souls beneath, the perfect young bodies, unselfconscious, accepting, knowing no idea of shame. I heard you speak to each other, telling each other of your love, your voices unhesitant, untainted by cynicism, unrestrained by any fear of hurt or rejection. Yours was a world which made sense in and of itself, which needed no further explanation, no philosophy, no religion, no formulae of physics or mathematics to bring order out of chaos. Love had taken you and led you by the hand out of uncertainty, loneliness and longing into a blessedness beyond my imagination. Was it that that your discoverer had been unable to tolerate? Was this never about money or scandal, but simply the horror of a dark soul when presented with a light he could not bear, a paradise he had no choice but to destroy?

I put the photographs into a paper bag and got up from my chair. I checked my matches were in my pocket. Outside the shed in the gardens was a brazier for burning litter left by careless visitors. There I would watch them burn until the last fragment was consumed.

TWENTY

I walked from the station through the quiet suburb where you lived to the modest semi-detached you called home. Or did you really think of it that way? I never recall you using that word. The lady who answered the door smiled.

'Mr Harris? Please come in. My sister and I are just having some tea.'

Your aunt who had been at the funeral, for such I assumed her to be, had shed her crow-like appearance and held herself upright, her movements quick and decisive and her voice clear and firm. At the same time there was a warmth in her manner which, after my meetings with other members of your family, came as something of a surprise. She wore a neatly tailored suit over a shimmering green blouse and a silk scarf. Her hair, whose whiteness she made no attempt to conceal though it prematurely aged her, was tied neatly in a bun.

So at last I was face to face with your mother. Yet my first impressions were not of her but of the huge beige sofa on which she sat, taking up nearly all of one wall. Where was your piano? Opposite the sofa wall I registered the solid wood mantel clock beneath three flying wall ducks which dominated a pale-tiled mantelpiece over a hooded flue gas fire. I remember that although it was a warm day the fire was lit. Your aunt resumed her place on one of the two armchairs, indicating the other to me. At last I could observe your mother. She did not rise. She looked me up and down. Her face was set tight and her lips pursed. Unlike your aunt's, her apparel was haphazard, a long check skirt and green jacket over a blue shirt in coarse material, the whole suggesting she had picked up the first things at hand on rising.

I leaned forward, encouraged by a gentle nod from your aunt.

'Mrs Harvey, I wanted to say how sorry I am for your loss. It was an awful shock to all of us. I did have a chance to meet your husband when he came down to see us. I told him what a pleasure it was to teach Simon, how well he was doing.'

There was no response. Your aunt rose and poured tea into the three tiny china cups from the set in front of the sofa.

'I take it you would like some tea, Mr Harris, and a biscuit?'

'Thank you.'

She handed me the cup and plate with a ginger biscuit. Then she turned back to your mother, placing her cup into her hand.

'Here you are, Catherine, and don't forget your pill.'

There was a little brown bottle on the tray. Obediently she took a pill from your aunt's outstretched hand and swallowed it with a mouthful of tea. It was time for me to soldier on. I took a deep breath.

'Er, Mrs Harvey, I should explain why I am here. We are putting together a little tribute for Simon for the college magazine. I was wondering if it would be possible to know a bit about his early life. Also if you have any photos, when he was a child. Or even as a baby. Family holidays, you know. And certificates, prizes, anything like that. Also, about his music. He was very active at college in music. How he got started, I mean. And…'

I dried up. There was no point in trying to continue. It was not hostility, exactly. She just seemed to be elsewhere. She was clearly not yet ready to talk. It was beginning to look as if I had had a wasted journey. But that was the least of my problems. Somehow I had to extricate myself from that frozen tableau and from the house altogether and I had not the slightest idea how to do it. Like a guardian angel your aunt intervened, in a tone of practised authority.

'Mr Harris, perhaps you would like me to show you round. You might want to visit the bathroom anyway, before you go.'

I followed her out of the room. She led the way up the stairs. I had not imagined there would be anything in the house worth showing a visitor. That proved to be the case. Three tidy bedrooms, reassuringly bland prints of pastoral scenes on all the walls, a scrupulously clean bathroom. One of the bedrooms was a small single, which I assumed had been yours. But there was nothing in it to suggest that an adolescent boy had ever been near it to cast over it his own special aura of chaotic exploration. It was a neutral space, ready to receive any guest at any time and to offend none. After descending the stairs I made straight for the front door, afraid lest the tight knot in my stomach might make me retch.

'I think I had better be off,' I muttered to my guide.

'Of course. I'll see you out.'

She raised her voice and directed it towards the front room. 'Catherine, our visitor is leaving. Do you want to come and say goodbye?'

We were already outside on the doorstep. Your mother came out of the front room and stood inside the hallway. Her face had at last changed, had begun to register something from within. For the first time I saw a slight mobility in it, a trembling of the upper lip and a droop in the corner of the eyelids. She said nothing.

So, what was I doing there? It was true, what I had said about the college magazine. The editor, an earnest third year with thick glasses and nervous manner, had come to see me the day after my excursion on the river with Alban to ask if I had any useful material for a tribute article. I told him what little I knew. Then to my own surprise I said something which was not true at the time, that I was due to visit your parents soon and could ask them if they had anything in the house they could show me or perhaps even lend me. They could also tell more than I knew about your childhood. The editor was delighted and bustled out. I imagined him in later life, scurrying around the office of a Fleet Street paper, a pencil behind each ear, desperate to impress his editor with his latest scoop.

So what was I thinking? I had not enjoyed the visits of your father and brother, nor the funeral. Nothing in the attitude of your family then had encouraged me to want to develop an acquaintance with them. I knew the men were impervious to grief, in their different ways. But what about your mother? I had only seen her from a distance. She was not well, so your father had said. Surely she would have recovered a little by now, just enough to show some reaction. Was that what I wanted, needed to see, from those who had raised you from infancy to the day you first appeared timidly at my door to be interviewed?

It was your father who answered the telephone, his voice calm and detached as before. He agreed, readily enough but with neither enthusiasm nor hostility, to my suggestion for a visit, asking me to wait while he took down the details of the day and time I proposed. It was like making an appointment with a dentist.

'I'll walk with you to the station,' your aunt whispered to me. 'The exercise will do me good.' She turned round to call out to your mother. 'Will you be all right on your own for a few minutes, Catherine? I'm just going to show Mr Harris the shortcut to the station.' Your mother stood silent and motionless in the hallway. Your aunt shut the door firmly on her and joined me on the pavement. She set a brisk pace with which I had some difficulty in keeping up.

'I am sorry about your visit,' she said, after a minute, with no sign of shortness of breath. 'I hope you don't feel it was a waste of time. She is having a bad day today. I am with her most of the time.'

'I thought Mr Harvey might have been there. I spoke to him to arrange the visit. He made a note of the date and time.'

'That doesn't mean he ever intended to be there. He knew I would be. He's a creature of habit. Visitors never get in the way of his routine. Perhaps I can fill in some of the gaps for you, while we walk. You will have noticed something about the house. Or rather noticed that there is nothing worth noticing.'

So that was why she had shown me round. It was not just to get us both out of that room.

'Yes. Nothing at all about Simon. It's as if he never lived there. I thought at least his piano would still be somewhere.'

'It was in that room where we had tea. She sold it when he left to go to college. Filled the space with that awful sofa. There were photos of him. All the things you asked about. They've all gone. I have no idea what happened to them. I was shocked when I realised. She never mentions him now. Never even acknowledges him. She refused to talk to the priest about the funeral arrangements. Left all that to me and her husband. I have some photos of Simon at my house. I kept a sort of scrapbook over the years. Reports in the local paper about his school prizes, and getting his place at Oxford. I can let you have them, if that would help.'

'Yes, I'd like to see them. Did they have a falling out, he and his mother?'

'Actually from the day he was born. You must not think too badly of her. She is really a very sick woman. She takes antidepressants. She never got over... you see, she was totally convinced her second child would be a girl. She had prayed for it. She thought she and God had an agreement. I am sorry if these words are offensive to you. I am not a religious person. I had to keep a close eye on her. I was made a widow soon after my marriage and we had no children of our own. So I had time to spare. As her elder sister I felt a sense of duty towards her. I would follow her to the shops. Sometimes when she pushed Simon there in the pram she would leave it behind, make to come home alone carrying her shopping bag. I had to call out to her to remind her, make it look as if I had followed her by chance. She would pretend to be shocked at her forgetfulness. I tried talking to her about it. She admitted to me one day that she had done it deliberately, so someone would take him and look after him better than she could, so she said. These days, well, there are people who can help with this sort of thing. But not then.'

'Was it always like that?'

'No. She seemed to get better in later years. Started to take an interest in him. If anything it was too much the other way. Especially with the music. She encouraged that from the start. Sent him to good teachers. Made him practise for hours. She would get him to play for people when they came round. She was very proud of him. They actually became close, in a funny sort of way. Went to church together. Then he became an altar boy. She was delighted about that.'

'So what happened?'

'He grew up. That's what happened. Not her little boy any more. Now he was a young man, beautiful and secretive. He still played but only for himself. He refused to play if she was there. He stopped going to church. She couldn't take it.'

'But all boys grow up eventually. They have to distance themselves, find their own way. I'm not a parent and never will be. But surely it is something parents have to get used to.'

'Some do and some don't. With Tom, his brother, it was different. She never took much notice of him. Always let him do what he wanted and never expected much. She worships him now. He does so much for them. Pays for their holidays. He bought them a little place in Spain. A holiday home. They go there every year.'

'What about Mr Harvey? I mean, how did he react to his wife's behaviour over the years?'

She looked up at me with a smile in her eyes. 'You've met him.'

'Just the once.'

'Catherine is the youngest. My elder sister and I were already married when the war started. My husband was killed on D-Day, on the Normandy beaches. My elder sister's husband came back from the war as a hero. Lots of medals and decorations. They went over to Canada and did very well for themselves. Catherine met Reginald just before the war. He went off to North Africa to fight Rommel, and we three girls were put to work in armaments. They married as soon as he returned. She had never had a chance to get to know him. The truth is, nobody knows him. It's like he has a suit of armour on all the time. I saw a lot of both of them, watched their children grow up. He took little interest in either of them. He never had time for Simon. Hated all that business about church and music. Regards them as weaknesses, tolerable in a woman but not in a man. He wasn't even bothered when Simon got into Oxford. By then it was Tom who had his attention. He was like his father, only much more ambitious. He started to do well for himself down in London, with his law practice. That was when Reginald began to take an interest in Tom. Talked all the time to anyone who would listen about how well Tom was doing, how much money he was making. Apart from that, Reginald just goes to work, comes home, reads the paper. Never reads a book. Watches the television a bit, then goes to bed. That's it. No hobbies. He has a couple of drinking mates he sees once a week. They were in the army together. That's where he'll be now. It's his day to meet up with them after work and nothing's allowed to disturb that.'

'Drinking mates?'

'Yes, he drinks, but not much. Never gets drunk.'

'Does he drink at home?'

Her eyes widened. 'A strange question, Mr Harris.'

'I'm sorry. I am being too nosy. I thought for a moment it might have been important but it's not. Not now.'

'If you thought it was important then it must be. He takes a little whisky most evenings. Blend. Not expensive single malt or anything like that. He would have offered you some if he had been at home to meet you. I tried it once. Found it disgusting. Made me want to throw up. She likes sherry. Me, I have to confess to a penchant for gin, but only when I'm on my own. Tom's a beer and wine man, to the best of my knowledge. So there you have it, for what it's worth. All the family drinking habits. You've met Tom?'

'Yes. Again, very briefly. He came to college to pick up Simon's stuff. Told me he was too busy to attend the funeral. I asked him if the family wouldn't mind if I went. He said that would be fine.'

'So you were there? I didn't see you.'

'I kept a respectful distance. I was at the back in church. I didn't go to the grave. It would have been different if I had known you all before, but just appearing there as a stranger at a time like that...'

'I understand. Kind of you to come, and to behave so discreetly. You're a gentleman, Mr Harris. Yes, Tom is always busy. He's always been that way. It goes back to the family history. Their first house belonged to our mother. When she died the three of us inherited it. But I already had one and my elder sister was out in Canada and doing fine. She helped Simon out with some money when he started at college. So we let Catherine take over as sole owner of the house. It was a foundation for a good start in married life. But they rather wasted it. They sold it to buy a business which failed. So Tom was very focussed on restoring the family finances. That's understandable. When he succeeded, you can imagine how relieved and thankful his parents were. What was your impression of Tom?'

'Not really my type. Nor me his. I'm an academic, shut up in my ivory tower. He's out making money to pay taxes to pay for the likes of me. I admire him for what he's done. I could never have done anything like that. But...'

'But what...?'

'I can understand that he and his brother were chalk and cheese. But when a younger brother dies like that, I would have thought he would show a bit more of a reaction.'

She nodded. 'Yes. They're not exactly an emotional family, not outwardly. But everybody grieves in their own way.'

'That's what the priest said. I had a quick chat with him after the funeral.'

We had reached the station. She stopped and turned to me.

'I will write to you and send you some things about Simon for your tribute. I think that's a wonderful idea. And you will have my address and telephone number from my letter. My name is Monica, though I was always known as Molly for some reason. You can call me Molly. Molly Sanders. That was my husband's name. If you want to contact me at any time about Simon, or about what happened to him, please do. I was very fond of him, you see. I loved him, you can say. I don't know if he ever really knew how much. I'm from a generation who never learned to show their feelings.'

Her eyes were misty. On an impulse which took me by surprise but which she accepted as if it were the most natural thing in the world, I took her hand and kissed it.

'I'm Alan,' I said. 'And I would like us to keep in touch. And thank you for helping me out today.'

My gratitude was heartfelt. I hoped she would register how much.

She waved as I turned away and into the booking hall.

TWENTY-ONE

I had had even less success with your mother than with your father. What is it about me and parents?

It has to be because I can barely remember either of mine. I had last seen my mother the day I left for boarding school. The aunt who took me to the station to see me off wrote me a letter over two years later, addressed to the school. I had not been back home in the meantime, not even during school holidays. The city was still deemed unsafe. In her letter my aunt explained why my mother had not written to me. It had all been too much for her, my father's death, the factory work, the bombs. She had fallen ill with pneumonia. She was recovering but was still too ill for me to return home.

Another letter followed after a further year. I was to be happy for her. She had met a soldier and fallen in love. An American. A GI. Not just any GI but an officer. They were already on their way to Texas. She was one of thousands of GI brides. I was not angry or upset. I had almost forgotten her.

I returned home at last as the war approached its end, and attended a sixth form college as a day pupil. The remaining aunts had died or dispersed, leaving the one who had written to me in sole charge of the house. To the disappointment of my teachers at Fidelis College I had decided against the priesthood. An academic career seemed the next best thing.

I did not share the main obsession of my fellow students, which was with the girls' school nearby. My school friends would meet the girls on the street corners and make arrangements for a Saturday night rendezvous, in groups or couples. I would never have dared to go near any of the girls. But to my surprise some of them approached me, finding in me someone in whom they could confide. I had no idea why. Perhaps it was because they realised I was an outsider. I knew their boyfriends but I was not in competition with them. I would listen and sometimes sit with one of the girls on a park bench while she cried, offering her a crumpled handkerchief. They only came to me in times of crisis. Their boyfriends were seeing someone else. What had they done wrong? How could they continue to live? I had nothing useful to offer them, other than a sympathetic grunt and the patience to wait while they talked, with a fluency and vocabulary far richer than any I or my fellow pupils could have summoned. Somehow it seemed to be enough for them. In most cases they got back with their boyfriends, the misunderstandings were cleared up and I never heard from them again. But from those days I had inherited a memory. Not so much of words or voices as of a facial expression. I had just been reminded of it, in the face of your mother as she stood in the hallway, moments before the door shut on her.

The expression of a rejected lover.

As the rhythm of the train returning me to Oxford soothed me and my eyes began to close, I let my thoughts drift about to see if they could find an anchor on their own, without my over-analytical brain disrupting them. *Clippety-clap, clippety-clap.* The wheels rattling over the track. *Whisky and pills. Whisky and pills.* The little brown bottle on the tea tray. Whisky, the bottles unseen, in the cupboard. Cheap blend. He would have offered me one if I had been there. I would have refused, politely. Molly had tried it once and found it disgusting. Nobody liked it, apart from your father.

Certainly not you. But it was whisky which had killed you. That and the pills, from a little brown bottle, from a pharmacy, with the label scraped off. A bottle like that one on the tea tray.

So now I knew where the whisky and the pills had come from. Your father might have gone to the cupboard one day and wondered whether a bottle had gone missing. But perhaps he had been mistaken. He did not keep a strict count. Why should he, when nobody else drank the stuff? He was just getting older and more forgetful. It happened to everybody. So the bottle found its way into your luggage at the beginning of a new term and was hidden away in your room until needed. As for the pills, that would have been trickier. It would have been easy enough to salvage one of your mother's empty bottles from the rubbish. But siphoning the pills from the new bottles, one or two at a time every now and then so as not to arouse suspicion, that would have taken time and patience.

So you had been planning it for a long time. Maybe since before you met Alban. Planning, but not necessarily intending. Not from the beginning. You would have known in your early teens that you were different, not just going through a phase. One day, whatever changes in the law were being discussed, however attitudes were said to be changing, you feared it would not be enough. You would still be the outsider you had always been, only now doubly so. The time might come when you could no longer face life in this world. You would be prepared.

Meeting Alban did not change that. Alban was different. He could live with the man he was, have a future, come to terms, make whatever compromises would be needed. You could not. You could not live a lie or even a half-truth. There was a danger that you would drag Alban down with you into the maelstrom of your own emotions and conflicts. You had to set your lover free. And the only way you could be sure of doing that was to set yourself free, once and for all, no going back. There was of course a period of uncertainty, maybe even of hope. Of wondering whether with Alban's help you could after all make it through, find a place within and without where you could both live your lives. But the tipping point came with those photographs. It did not matter what anonymous homophobic bully or prurient prankster had taken them. You were being watched. You had been given a message. You are different. We cannot accept you. We have the power to destroy you.

TWENTY-TWO

A week later I had a phone call from Molly. She had put together a number of papers and photographs which I might find useful for our tribute. She proposed that instead of entrusting the material to the post she would, if I agreed, bring it down in person. Then, if I could spare the time, I could show her round. She had never been to Oxford before. She had already taken the liberty of booking a room at a little hotel in the Iffley Road.

We met at a coffee shop in the High. When I arrived she was already seated by the window, a pot of coffee, a tray of biscuits and two plates and cups in front of her.

'I've already ordered, as you see,' she said, rising to shake my hand. 'Somehow I knew you would be punctual to the minute.'

I sat down opposite her. She was smartly dressed in a green velvet suit with matching necktie. She wore sturdy leather walking boots. I poured the coffee.

'It's good to see you again,' I said, as warmly as I could. I hoped she could see through my natural reserve to know that I really meant it.

'And I'm pleased to see you, especially after that awful visit you had. I am sorry about that. I could have warned you off. But I only learned that morning that you were coming. I told you it was his day to be with his drinking pals. But I think he might have found another pretext, if it had been another day. I suspect he finds you intimidating. Not just you. Anybody in any sort of position. And he has no small talk.'

'I did notice. I'm much the same. You don't find me intimidating, do you?'

'Not at all, even though I suppose I should. I'm usually the one who intimidates. I'm so used to saying what I think. All these years of living on my own, and now having to deal with my sister every day. I'm long past the stage when I take any nonsense, least of all from myself. You know, right from the start I had a feeling you and I would get on.'

'Me, too. I'm sorry it was such a tragic event that led us to meet. But I am grateful to you. Truly.'

'For what?'

'For being there to rescue me. When your sister just sat there and said nothing, I had no idea how to get out of it.'

She took a sip of coffee. 'Alan, do you mind awfully if I smoke? I know it's a terrible habit and I'm sure you disapprove.'

'Not at all. Go ahead.'

She took a silver cigarette case and lighter out of her leather handbag. She placed the tip of a cigarette gently between her lips and waited. A memory flickered, of a rare wartime school trip, courtesy of a kindly teacher who was a movie buff, to a fleapit in the nearest town. A Humphrey Bogart film was showing. Now I had a role to play. I picked up the lighter, which was far heavier than I expected. I flicked the flint inexpertly and was relieved to see the blue flame emerge hesitantly. I leaned forward. She drew the smoke into her lungs and sighed.

'Thank God,' she said. 'Now you know the full extent of my vices. I do not need or wish to know the extent of yours.'

A line from the same movie? If not, it would have fitted. The way she delivered it reminded me of Lauren Bacall, as she surely intended.

'Lady, believe me, you are absolutely right not to want to know.' I hoped it sounded just a bit like Bogart. I never had any talent for mimicry. 'Actually,' I went on in my normal voice, 'I am sorry to disappoint you but I don't have any. Vices, that is. So, what would you like to see first?'

'Actually, if you don't mind, I prefer to visit places on my own. The tourist bits, I mean. I've bought a guidebook. But there is one place where only you can take me. And as soon as we've had coffee I'd like to go there.'

'Is this it?'

We were at the same bend in the river where I had taken Alban. This time we had gone on foot, through the Parks. I was beginning to feel like a tourist guide, delivering a routine address to a series of visitors and trying to make it sound fresh each time.

'Yes. Near enough. His punt was found here. His body floated downstream until it came to a mill. It was trapped there.'

'What was in the punt?'

'An empty bottle of whisky and a little pill bottle. Also empty.'

She nodded slowly. 'I see. The paper local to us didn't give much detail. Just said an overdose.'

'That's right. But...'

'Go on. I'm a grown-up woman. It may look as if I've had a sheltered life but that's only on the surface. If you know anything else, tell me. That's the real reason why I wanted to see this place.'

'The immediate cause of death was drowning. The pills and whisky established his intent to kill himself.'

'So on the day it happened he got hold of a punt. How?'

'Very easily. He booked one of our college punts. They're usually all taken out on summer afternoons.'

'Do you have to book in advance?'

'Not necessarily. Some times are more popular than others. Friday evenings, for example. But if there's one free, you can take it out without prior notice. Just enter your name in the book against the number of the punt. Then you go and pick it up. The earliest you can book is first thing in the morning, just after breakfast.'

'So, there's no way of knowing if he booked it in advance or at the time. It could have been on impulse.'

'Yes.'

'And he took it out on his own.'

'Yes. One of the other undergraduates saw him.'

'And that is the sort of thing which would be noticed.'

'Yes. Normally you go out in company. Punting on your own is a sign you're a social loser, so I'm told.'

'And this boy wouldn't have seen what he had with him.'

'No. The stuff was in a bag. Hidden under a seat, I imagine.'

'And nobody saw him moor up here.'

'No.'

'He drank the whisky and took the pills. Then he entered the water. Still alive at that point.'

She frowned, concentrating on every detail I was telling her, trying to assemble the whole picture in her head.

'Yes. I don't know if he could swim, but in that state he would not have been able to. He would have been barely conscious.'

'He could swim. He used to go to the baths at Southport when he was younger. That's all?'

'Yes.'

It wasn't, of course. But I was sworn to secrecy about the photographs.

'No note,' she continued, 'according to the paper. But a clear intent to kill himself. The whisky and pills prove that.' She spoke as if to herself. Then she turned to me. 'Can we walk along the path a little? I need to breathe.'

She took my arm as we walked, avoiding the roots of giant willows that bent and dipped into the water. Punts glided back and forth, bringing near and bearing away the cheerful chatter of their occupants.

'So, Alan, what do you think drove him to it?'

I was still wondering what I could say in reply when she spoke again.

'Before you answer, if there are confidences you feel obliged to honour, then I respect you for that. So let me rephrase the question in a way which may get you off the hook. Do you think it had something to do with his homosexuality?'

I stumbled, my foot grazing against a root which reared up before me like a surprised snake. She clutched my arm tightly to prevent me falling.

'I am very sorry, Alan, I shouldn't have sprung that on you like that. But you did know, I think.'

'Yes, I knew.'

'He came to see me, during the last vacation, just before returning here. He told me he had fallen in love with a wonderful person. A fellow student. His whole life was transformed. He didn't need to tell me that. I could tell just from the look in his eyes. I had never seen him so happy. He said the person he loved was a boy his own age, and he loved him in return. He said I mustn't think it was just a phase. For him it was the real thing. He knew that was the way it was with him, and always would be. He said he wanted all his family to know but he had chosen me to be the first. I advised him not to tell anybody else just yet. Perhaps there was something I could do to prepare the ground, I told him. I promised to try. The truth is that I was at a loss to know how to help him. I knew his parents would never accept it, whatever anybody said or did. I agonised over what to do next. My inclination was to try to persuade him not to tell them. It was probably too late anyway for his mother to understand. And I could see no point in him telling his father, when he had shown so little interest in Simon over the years. So why cause unnecessary disruption, most of all to his own peace of mind? After many days of turning it all over in my mind, and many sleepless nights, I decided to talk to Simon again and tell him what I had concluded. If he was still adamant, then I would keep my promise and speak to his parents first. But we never had the chance to talk again. That time he told me was the last time I ever saw him.'

'I had the same impression, that he was very happy. But I think the idea of suicide had come to him before. Perhaps a long time before. When he first realised he was different. It all comes back to those bottles. He could have bought the whisky anywhere, of course, though I have never heard of any undergraduate having blend whisky in his room. But the real problem was the pills. They were prescription only. Then when I went to the house and met you and his mother there, I understood.'

'That he got the whisky and the pills from the house.'

'Yes. Easy to slip a bottle of the whisky into his luggage and his father would probably not notice. But he would have had to take the pills one at a time and hide them, over a long period, so his mother would not realise.'

'You think he made a secret store, some time ago, in case one day he might decide he needed them.'

'Yes.'

'So why, when he had found happiness at last, would he suddenly make that fateful decision? Did his lover reject him?'

'No. I've met him. Since Simon's death. It was as much a shock to him as to any of us.'

'But something else. Some sort of trigger? I think you are hiding something, Alan. But that's all right. You have your reasons. You have given someone your word and I respect that. Let's go back now.'

We walked back in silence. When we reached the High, she stopped and took my hand.

'This is where I go solo, Alan. As I said, I like to be on my own when I'm doing the sights. So I'll let you go back to your duties. Thank you for your time and the walk. I'll send the stuff I've brought about him round to your college. It'll be there later today. I think I'll be doing some grieving as well as sightseeing. I need to be on my own for that. I don't like people to see me when I'm crying. I'm old-fashioned like that.'

'Good to know that someone in the family can grieve.'

She leaned forward and kissed my cheek. As I turned to leave she caught my sleeve. I turned back.

'Oh, just one thing you might want to think about,' she said, lowering her voice. 'Your theory about the pills, that he accumulated them secretly over a long period, is very good. The only problem is that it can't be true. You see, I monitor every pill she takes. I have done for years. She doesn't like to leave the house and hates going to the shops. So she authorises me to collect her prescriptions. I count every pill that comes into the house and watch her as she takes them. One pill when

I arrive, one with her lunch and one before I leave. If she took one when I wasn't there I would know about it. But one whole new bottle went missing. I'd got it from the chemist the day before. This was not long ago. Just before he came up for the start of this term, not long after he talked to me about his new love. The bottle was still unopened. She couldn't find it anywhere. She told me she must have thrown it out with the rubbish. I searched the house myself, from top to bottom. Then I went out to get a replacement. So, Professor, tell me this. How did that lost bottle end up a couple of weeks later, empty, in that punt, the contents in my nephew's stomach? And assuming he took it with him along with the whisky, why did he do that just after telling me all about his new-found happiness? You're a clever man. That's why you're here. So if you can figure it out you know where to find me.'

TWENTY-THREE

I was awakened by Max's unmistakable knock. At first I was unsure where I was. I had dozed off in my armchair, the evening after meeting Molly. There were thoughts, or questions, revolving in my mind. But now that Max had interrupted me I could not recall them. Were they about a problem in my researches, or something a student had raised with me in a tutorial? Or was it to do with the last words Molly had said to me, about figuring something out? Never mind. If it was important it would come back to me later. I called for him to enter.

'Er, Mr Harris...' Despite our having been brought closer together through our recent adventure with Alban I knew there was no point in asking him to call me by my first name. He had stepped inside the room and drawn himself up to his full height.

'Mr Harris, I was wondering if you would do me the honour of joining me for a nightcap in the lodge. Round the back. It's nice and peaceful there this time of night, until they start coming back from the pubs.'

I was relieved he did not want to take me for another drive.

'Yes, Max. I'm the one who'd be honoured. I'd love to.'

He clicked his heels, his expression of respectful dignity unaltered, and marched out. I followed him across the quad, into the lodge and behind a screen at the back. Here was Max's private domain, a tiny space with a single knee-high cupboard. As he opened the cupboard with the air of a priest unveiling the Blessed Sacrament at Mass I could see that it contained a bottle of brandy, an expensive brand, probably a present from a student he had helped to extricate from a particularly tricky hole. There were no glasses. He chose two of the cleaner mugs into which to pour the brandy. He invited me to take the only chair which could fit into the space. He stood upright by the cupboard as if to defend it against all comers.

'There's something I wanted to explain, Mr Harris, about that young man and how all that business came about.'

'There's no need, Max. You did the right thing and we're both very grateful.'

'How is he now?'

'He's on the mend, thanks to you. God knows what state he would be in by now if he had just wandered off and you hadn't stepped in and looked after him. You can be proud of what you did.'

'Thank you. But there's still something I wanted you to know. I suppose you're wondering how I knew they were friends, the one who died and the one I took in. I knew they were more than just friends, you see. They were at the main gate, still inside, just before I was due to come out and close it. It was midnight. There was nobody at the counter. I was in here, sitting where you are. I was having a little doze, actually. Their voices woke me up. I looked round. I could see them but they couldn't see me. He, the one I took in, was leaving. So they were saying goodnight to each other. And more than saying goodnight. Kissing. Holding each other. I could have reported them for misconduct on college premises. Actually, that is what I should have done.'

'So, why didn't you?'

He took a long sip of brandy.

'I'm going to tell you something nobody else in college knows, Mr Harris. My son died in a car accident. Well, yes, that is known. He was sixteen. What you and others don't know is that he was like those two. He had told me. I'm ashamed of what I did, Mr Harris. Sick and ashamed. It was the way I'd been raised. Very strict and traditional. I'd been brought up to think it was a sin beyond all redemption. I told him to get out of the house and never come back. His mother was there. She took his side. They both packed and left. We had a cottage in Devon in those days. They were going to go there. They left in the middle of the night, after a terrible row between my wife and me. He said nothing, just watched and waited for us to finish. She took him in our car. On the way, a lorry overturned in front of them. They never had a chance. I blamed myself. I thought he would be punished in some way. But when the tragedy happened I realised that I was the one being punished. It was my fault, you see. I had thrown them out. I know now that I would have gone to see them after a few days. To apologise. To tell them I loved them, despite everything. To say I would understand if they wanted nothing more to do with me. But I never had the chance. Ever since then I've tried to make it up by helping other young people, help them find the future he never had, because of me. That's why I took this job. You wouldn't believe the problems they bring to me, and if I can sort them out I do. And when I saw those two, and later when I knew the young man was in trouble when I saw him in the street… I'm sorry if I scared him, but I had to follow him and try to help if I could.'

His voice was breaking. I stood up and put my hand on his shoulder.

'I'm glad to know the young man is better now,' he continued, almost sobbing. 'But if there is anything else I can do, you just let me know. You will do that, won't you, sir? Won't you, Mr Harris? Anything at all. Just say the word.'

He sat down, his head in his hands, his shoulders shaking. 'I will, Max. I promise.'

TWENTY-FOUR

An Oxford summer at its seductive best descended on us, cool river breezes and dappled shades from gigantic trees easing any discomfort from the heat. I took long walks along the riverbank and in the University Parks, listening to the shouts and the thwack of bat on ball from the cricket ground, the swish of punts through the water, the earnest chatter from huddled groups on the grass, the sense of growing tension as the date of finals approached. I could just have basked in it all, as I had always done before. But again and again I was drawn back to that same place where your punt had been moored.

One day, to my totally unreasonable irritation, I saw that another punt had been moored at exactly the same spot. It was occupied by a young couple. The girl wore a floral-patterned summer dress and wide-brimmed straw hat. From the bank where I stood I could not see her face. Her companion was dressed casually, in a red short-sleeved shirt and faded blue jeans. He was leaning over the side of the punt, dangling what looked like a bottle of champagne in the slow current, trying, I presumed, to chill it to the desired temperature. They were both laughing. I guessed that the bottle they were trying to cool was already their second.

'Further out,' she called. 'It's deeper there. It flows faster. It'll be cooler. You'll never chill it that way. Go on. Lean further out.'

He stretched out, his arms fully extended, half his body out of the punt.

'Further, further!' she yelled. The punt rocked slightly in the waves he was creating.

'I can't,' he gasped. 'I'll lose the bottle.'

'If you do you can go in after it. At least that'll make it nice and cool. Anyway, you always were a drip.' She shrieked with laughter.

He grabbed the sides and pushed himself back into the punt, the bottle still in his hand. He pushed off the cork and it flew away into the river, the top of the bottle foaming as he handed it to her. She squealed as the foam tickled her nostrils.

I walked off before they could realise they had been spotted. I was furious. They had spoiled the scene for me. Could they not sense that it was a hallowed spot and that their frivolity was blasphemy?

By the late evening, when I finally got back to college, I had walked for miles. My desk was full. There were letters to write, essays to mark, lecture notes to prepare. After an hour I had made no progress with any of those tasks. But I had drawn a diagram. The random thoughts which had been drifting through my mind when Max interrupted my doze had finally coalesced. Not into the solution of a problem but into a pattern of questions.

My diagram consisted of four questions at four points of the compass.

First question, at the top. Why whisky and pills? Why not just stones in your pockets, Virginia Woolf style?

Second question, to the right. Why no note? There was someone dear to you. You were leaving him behind. Did you really have nothing to say to him before you went?

Third question, to the left. Why death by water? Whisky and pills would work as well in the quiet of your locked room or any secluded spot.

Fourth question, underneath. If water was your chosen medium, why the punt to take you there? There was a path leading to the spot where you had moored.

From each question I had drawn a straight line, all of them meeting at a point in the middle. I drew a circle around the point. What did it signify? What was missing? What should go into the circle that would draw the lines into itself and solve the puzzle?

But of course there was no puzzle. Not in my questions, nor in the one Molly had put to me and which had turned itself over in my mind repeatedly ever since. They were only manifestations of the affliction which is the curse of all of my profession and my cast of thinking, the need to search for rational explanations even where there can be none. Who, and least of all I, could possibly presume to fathom the workings of a mind bent on self-destruction? It was an act which would take far more courage than I would ever have. Why should it not also involve imagination, careful planning over a long period, the laying of a false trail leading others to shock and surprise at an act so at odds with the appearance of happiness, a desire to construct an elaborate and memorable final scene which only poetry can properly describe? Shakespeare would have understood. Nobody in *Hamlet* questions the way in which Ophelia stages her end or asks for a rational explanation for each of her actions. It is enough that the solemn music, at once grieving and consoling, of Gertrude's epitaph makes it unforgettable for all time. *There is a willow grows aslant a brook.* Was it her death you recalled as you planned it? Was that why it had to be in that place and in that way? Willows grow aslant the river where you died, and their leaves too are hoary in the glassy stream. Your garments too were heavy with their drink, until they pulled you to muddy death. Did you think that those who knew and loved you would soon forget you, but would never be able to forget the manner of your passing? Did you think that would be your only memorial?

TWENTY-FIVE

A year passed. I spent the long vacation researching for a new course of lectures I was planning, visiting Harvard and the Sorbonne. I returned to the gold and yellow opulence of an Oxford autumn, leaves thick and crunchy underfoot, a chill in the air which hastened and amplified the sound of the bells, a higher and faster flow in the river, a batch of fresh faces at my tutorials, everywhere a sense of new energy and purpose. The college revived itself as it did every year, fresh coats of paint on the doors, another layer of grime removed from the most ancient of the walls, the trees and shrubs in the gardens lovingly and sparingly pruned. The fellows re-greeted each other and exchanged subdued chat (it would not do to sound like the excited undergraduates) about their vacation activities, the wealthier not failing to mention their holidays in the Bahamas while the rest grumbled about the discomfort of their draughty cottages in remote rural retreats. The Master had at last shaken off the haunted look he had worn over the summer and welcomed us back as if we had been reported lost without hope of recovery in the jungles of the Amazon. Max proudly took up his position in the lodge to welcome the freshers and see they found their way to their rooms, taking careful note of which ones seemed likely to suffer most from early homesickness and so to need his paternal attention in the weeks ahead. It was as if the tragic events of the previous summer had never been. Alban still came to see me from time to time, though less frequently as the weeks went by and he found consolation in work and new friendships.

I too found relief in the return of reassuring routines. I was pleased that my new students seemed to fulfil the promise they had shown at their interviews. The course of lectures I had planned over the summer was well received. Hilary Term followed Michaelmas and brought severe frosts and some snow. I watched from my window as groups of students engaged in impromptu snowball fights, wondering if there had been anything like that in my day. Probably there had but I had not noticed. Like everything else it would have passed me by. If anybody had seen me watching now, would they have said I was smiling at last? Probably not. Some habits never die and new ones are hard to acquire. But inside I knew I was smiling, and that was enough for me.

Yes, things were proceeding smoothly enough, right up to the start of the new Trinity term and the anniversary of your death. Alban and I visited the spot where we had laid flowers and performed the same ceremony. We walked there and back together, in silence. When we came to the place in the meadows where our ways parted, we shook hands. I put my hand on his shoulder as he turned away. Probably he would come to see me once or twice in the weeks ahead, but already I sensed that our lives were diverging. That was as it should be. I had had time to prepare myself for the loneliness.

TWENTY-SIX

T hen everything changed again.

I was not to know that at the time. It was a routine matter, a bit of delayed tidying up of your affairs, nothing more. All I felt was my usual irritation at the prospect of having to make a visit to London.

I hate London. I go there as little as possible. Millions cram into its streets every day, all of them in the wrong place, all of them desperate to be somewhere else. Wherever it is they need to be, for work, for an appointment, for lunch, it is always miles from where they happen to find themselves. And they are always late, always impatient of anyone like me who prefers to be early and might want to take a moment to stop and stare.

As I was staring then, at the vast Victorian Gothic pile of the Law Courts on the other side of the Strand, relieved at last to be close to my destination. I had just emerged like a light-startled rodent from the Underground station, having been physically carried along several wrong corridors and up a similar number of wrong escalators, all this after a journey squeezed in the middle of a quartet of sweating young men in damp tight blue suits, yellow shirts and kipper ties. They ignored each other. I could not tell if they were colleagues bound for the same place or if they had just found each other by mutual recognition. They all had a practised knack of balance I could not manage, rocking on tiptoe while dextrously flipping the pages of their newspapers. I clung to whatever handhold I could find, my gaping mouth searching for any breath of air which might be passing, aware of the pitying looks the seated passengers reserved for an outsider. The moment I stepped out into the sunlight I was swept up again, this time by a crowd trying to enter the cavern whence I had just managed to emerge. I narrowly escaped being pushed back in, only succeeding by realising that I had to forget about Oxford manners and fight with arm and elbow for every inch of ground.

At last I was there, at the edge of the pavement. The river of humanity across which I had just fought my way was behind me and I was able to get my bearings. Just opposite the Courts, she had told me, then down a narrow lane, with the ancient Wig and Pen Club on the corner, through a courtyard, then the first door on the right. I spotted the lane, dark and inviting, and steeled myself for another bruising struggle to get across the pavement.

When I reached the lane I remembered that there is always another London if one can only take the time and patience to discover it, silent, hidden, waiting to be explored, too full of history and dignity to be anything other than contemptuous of the hurry and bustle beyond. The near deserted, shadowy, twisting lane and its dark-bricked, narrow-windowed uneven walls soothed my harassed soul. It was as if I had never left my Oxford refuge, as if my passage there through the press of bodies in the stifling subterranean tunnel to the swarms on the broad sunlit streets had been but a nightmare vision of the Last Judgement. Here, as in my home, tradition ruled. Staircases reminiscent of those in my college led up to barristers' chambers from uneven paving illuminated by shadowy lamps that would once have been gas, to be laboriously lit each evening by a man in a greasy leather cap and apron and holding a wax taper. Up those stairs there would still be scrolls and parchments and quill pens, however much they now had discreetly to take second place to electric typewriters and fax machines. The young lawyers might now wear sharp suits and freshly laundered shirts and speak the lexicon of modern business. But they would always be aware of the centuries-old weight of precedent and procedure, of hallowed turns of phrase and idiom.

She had rung me the day before. Her voice was clear, decisive, impossible to pin down as to age.

'Mr Harris? This is Mr Harvey's secretary. Thomas Harvey, of Harvey's Solicitors, Outer Temple. I'm calling you about Simon, your pupil. Mr Harvey's brother. Your pupil as was, I mean. I am talking to the right person?'

No, not pupil. But let that pass. 'Yes, I'm the one. I was his tutor.'

'Oh good. It's just about his stuff. Simon's, I mean. The legal aspects have all been sorted now. I'm sorry it's taken so long. I was wondering if you would like to come and collect his things. We've no room to store it here, you see. And there may be items you want to keep in the college. I've been told not to bother his parents. They'd be too upset.'

The speech sounded rehearsed, a piece of business to be despatched as soon as possible so she could get on with something more important. I had the impression she had a list of key points on a pad in front of her.

'Yes, thank you.' I hoped my annoyance did not show in my voice. She was only doing her job. And it would be a good idea to get this one remaining loose end sorted once and for all.

'I don't have a car and I don't drive,' I continued. 'I could come up by train and have a look at what's there. If there is anything which I think we ought to keep I can arrange for a courier to collect it. The rest you can dispose of locally. Would that be convenient?'

'Yes, that would be fine. I was just looking for a suitable date and time. How about next Wednesday at noon?'

'Yes, that would suit me. Can you give directions?'

To reach it I had to pass through those Dickensian squares and dimly lit staircases of the barristers' quarters to a small modern enclave of nondescript office buildings beyond. I was now in the area of the camp-followers, the workaday solicitors and providers of humdrum legal support services without whom the glamorous barristers with their dramatic court presentations and fees of several thousand pounds a day would have no work. The lift was cramped and creaked worryingly.

Stepping out of the lift I assumed I had got off at the wrong floor. There was a narrow corridor to either side with boxes and piles of papers stacked at random. Opposite the lift was an open door, beyond which I could see more boxes and papers but no furniture. Telephones, table lamps and a fax machine all sat forlornly on the bare wooden floor. Yet the name on the door confirmed I was in the right place.

'Mr Harris, is that you?' a familiar voice called out, softened by proximity and the absence of the harsh acoustic of telephone wire. 'Come on in. I'm just having some coffee. Will you have one?'

I stepped carefully into the room. It was a high, triple-windowed space which might once have accommodated a dozen people with room for a spacious desk for each, a comfortable seating area and a separate conference table at one end. But all that was supplied by my imagination. The whole of the floor space opposite the windows was taken up by yet more boxes and papers. I found her at last, crouching on the floor beneath the central window, a steaming kettle plugged into a socket by her right side. She was in the act of shaking instant coffee powder from a large jar into one of two cracked mugs by her feet, with no apparent attempt at measurement. A can of powdered milk was on the floor on her left side. There were no spoons that I could see.

She looked up. She wore a T-shirt, jeans and plimsolls, all dusty and stained. Her hands were white with dust. She wore a Mrs Mop-style grey flannel headscarf, though if that gave the appearance of a cleaner it was of one who had long since abandoned her task as hopeless. Mid-thirties, I guessed. She smiled, enjoying my obvious surprise.

'Actually, I wouldn't recommend the coffee. It's mostly dust and the milk is as bad. And the mugs are all I can find. Definitely not to be recommended. The stains have been there since Dodson and Fogg had these offices.' She smiled again, pleased I had obviously understood her literary joke. Her precise Home Counties diction and the reference were definitely not Mrs Mop. 'However, I need the caffeine and I am immune to all this place can throw at me. And I don't just mean the bugs and the dirt. I imagine coffee in an Oxford college is a rather different experience. We can go out for one later. The local inn does a reasonable espresso. I'll be ready for something much stronger by then.'

I was aware of an edge to her voice, a struggle between stoic coping in the spirit of the Blitz, about which perhaps her parents had told her, and an impulse to rush screaming around the room in a fit of total hysteria.

She stood up to shake hands, removing her headscarf in the process. Her hair was jet black and straight, expertly shaped to frame her cheekbones, the overall look severe but not intimidating. Tom Harvey had chosen her carefully, for more than her efficiency. She was tall and slim, attractive enough to put clients at ease but not so arresting as to distract either them or her colleagues. I imagined her in her smart, secretarial jacket, blouse and pencil skirt. Her outfit would exude not only efficiency but a reassuring, though not excessive, level of expenditure. A firm which could afford her would easily secure ample rewards for its clients without needing to stint on its own staff. That would have been the impression she had been trained to give. Until now, when skills and attributes of a quite different nature were required, ones for which she had not bargained when she had started work there. She sat down again in the same position.

'Sheila Black,' she continued. 'Tom's secretary. In a manner of speaking. I would invite you to have a seat, but as you see there isn't one to be had for love or money. And I won't ask you to join me on the floor. You don't want to spoil your nice suit. I'm sorry, I should have warned you to bring your decorating outfit. Not that we're redecorating, you understand, in case you were thinking that.'

'So you're moving offices,' I ventured, suspecting a much harsher truth. In the tense laugh which followed, the spirit of the Blitz was already close to forgotten.

'Moving? I suppose you could say that. From here to eternity. From being to non-being. If you're wondering where his lordship is, he's not here. It's just me, a ghost haunting the ruins. And after tomorrow, nothing. His brother's stuff is in that box over there by the door. Do what the hell you want with it. Set fire to it. Set fire to the whole place. Just give me a chance to get out first.'

'So the business…'

'Closed down. For good.'

'He never gave the slightest indication of that. He kept saying how busy he was. But that was some time ago.'

'He's been busy, I grant him that. But not exactly with earning a living. For fuck's sake, let's get out of here. We can come back for your stuff later.'

We were back in barrister land. The pub crouched in a dark corner of a miniature square. It was itself miniature, a single room with the bar along one side and plush red velvet seating along the other three sides beneath dark oak panels. There were no tables, only small round stands at chest height on which glasses could be placed by customers unable to find seating space. I imagined the self-congratulatory chatter and backslapping of the lawyers who would later crowd in, shouting their orders for the usual from the doorway. But it was still early and we were the only ones there. We huddled in a corner as far away from the bar as possible, though the young barman dressed like a croupier had disappeared into the back as soon as he had served us.

'So what happened?' I asked.

She took a long sip of gin and tonic. 'Do you want the whole truth or the edited version? Well, never mind, you'll get the lot. Whether you want it or not. But first I need another one of these.'

I walked over to the bar and called out for the barman, fearing my donnish tones, always suffused with a question whether there was one to be asked or not, would be insufficiently confident to gain his attention. He crept back sullenly, drying his hands on a paper towel.

'Same again?'

I nodded. I took our drinks back, a large gin for her with the tonic still in the bottle, and an espresso for me. This time she ignored the tonic and swallowed the gin in one gulp.

'He was actually a rather good lawyer. Tough and sharp. When sober. Best not to try to get any decisions out of him after three o'clock, though. He'd come over here about this time of day, saying he had to get to know his clients, essential to business, all that stuff. Sometimes he'd never come back until the next morning. My job was to front for him. Later it was to cover for him. Then sign for him. Then prepare and sign for him, stuff he never even saw, even when that was just a little bit illegal. I never did the accounts side of things, though. He kept all that to himself. Then the investigators came in. From the Law Society. There had been complaints from clients. Mostly about delays at first. Then more serious ones. About money they were owed not being passed on to them. They closed the business down. It was to protect clients' money. Then last week we had the formal decision. Struck off. Forbidden to practise law any more. The clients are suing him. There's nothing left in the business, as you saw. Only bills. The phones and the electricity are being cut off tomorrow. He had a flat in Islington and a little cottage in Suffolk for weekends. That was where he and I... Yes, we were lovers, I suppose you could say. Though love is not part of his vocabulary. That was soon after I first arrived. He kept me on, even after we had stopped sleeping together. He had to. I knew too many of his secrets. He's sold both those places. There are a lot of other debts, you see. He has nothing left to sell.'

'What about the place in Spain, for his parents?'

'You heard about that? That's sold too. Only they don't know yet. I only hope they don't try and go out there this year.'

'But didn't the proceeds pay his debts?'

'Hardly. It was the place in Spain that broke the camel's back. He borrowed heavily to buy it.'

'That explains it.'

'Explains what?'

'The money his brother gave him. It must have gone towards the Spanish property. I noticed it in one of his bank statements, when I was going through his stuff before passing it over to your boss. I was surprised to see a student handing over a fair sum to a lawyer, even if it was his brother. His aunt told me that another aunt, the one who had gone to Canada to live, helped Simon out with money when he first came up. I suppose Tom knew about it and said he would invest some of it on his behalf.'

'I don't know anything about that. As I told you, Tom handled all the accounts himself. Except that nobody in their right minds ever placed money with him for investment. All I know is that I'm out of a job. And by the end of the week I'll be homeless. Haven't paid my rent for over a year. And that's how long he hasn't been paying me, even though I was doing all his work on his behalf while he was in here drinking himself to oblivion and telling everybody about all his wonderful successes. He never even paid my fare for those trips. I only stayed with him out of loyalty. And to what? A phoney, a creep, a liar and a fraud. Not loyalty. Blind stupidity.'

'Where is he now?'

'A lawyer friend of his has a barge in Little Venice. The friend's away in America, for several years. Tom's house-sitting for him. Or barge-sitting, rather. I take his correspondence to him there. I leave it for him. Sometimes I wait and watch while he tears it up without reading it. Not that there is any these days. All dried up. He isn't dried up, of course. His friend left a huge quantity of booze on board. Tom's working his way through it.'

'And his car?'

Her laugh was shrill, close to the edge.

'His car? His? It was never his. Belongs to the same friend. No idea where it is now. I think his friend had a garage near the barge. I suppose it's there. I doubt if Tom has any reason to use it. Not that he's ever sober enough these days.'

Something she had said was nibbling at the corner of my mind.

'Trips?'

'Sorry?'

'You said something about trips. A few moments ago. He sent you somewhere but never paid your fare.'

'Yes. Oh, don't worry. It wasn't to Timbuktu, or anything like that. Just to your place, as a matter of fact. Oxford.'

'He had business there? Apart from what happened to his brother, I mean?'

'This was about his brother. He had no business contacts there.'

'I'm sorry, I'm getting confused. He came to see me in person. That was when he collected his brother's stuff.'

'That's right. After his brother died. This was before.'

I was staring into my empty coffee cup, rudely forgetting her presence.

'Mr Harris?' She waved her hand in front of my unfocussed eyes.

'I'm sorry, Sheila. My attention was wandering. That's what happens with eccentric bachelor dons. You'll have to excuse me. I was just wondering about what you said. Why would he send you to Oxford before his brother's death but come in person afterwards?'

'He couldn't send me to pick up his stuff, could he? I don't drive. And I never knew what was in those envelopes.'

'Envelopes?'

'God, you're like a bloody dog worrying at a bone. Do you never let go? He gave me some envelopes to deliver. Two visits, one envelope each. Obviously didn't want to trust them to the post. That's it. No big deal.'

'And you delivered them…'

'One of them to your college. To his brother. To Simon.'

I scrambled to my feet. 'Sorry, got to get to the gents,' I mumbled.

TWENTY-SEVEN

I rushed frantically into the single cramped cubicle, my chest heaving. I must not jump to conclusions, I told myself. It could have been anything. But you and he were leading separate lives. What connection was there between you to require the hand delivery of a document? Only that so-called investment, in the Spanish property. It might have been a legal paper to do with the purchase. He had not wanted to trust it to the post and he knew he could rely on Sheila. But why had he not even paid her expenses? If his business was already in such trouble, why bother to send a document to you about an investment which could never pay off? There could be other, perfectly innocent explanations. I had to get back to her before she was too drunk to tell me any more.

I returned to the bar very slowly, trying to fix a reassuring expression onto my face. She looked up in surprise, as if she had forgotten our conversation, even that I had been there with her. She had, as I feared, got herself another drink during my absence and nearly finished it. I sat down and took a deep breath.

'I want to ask you some more things. I'm sorry to take up more of your time. I am not a wealthy man. I live frugally and save most of my modest salary. I promise I will pay you everything your boss owes you from my own pocket, in return for your help. That is how important this is to me. Some of my questions might sound trivial but I have my reasons for asking.'

She sighed. 'Frankly, I don't give a shit about the money. Forget it. You don't miss what you never expected to get. But thanks for the thought. Look, if you've got something on him, whatever it is, then you have my full cooperation.'

Her slurred speech struggled with the last word but at last she spat it out.

'When did you deliver the envelope to his brother?'

'Not that long before he killed himself. I had to take it to your college and give it in person to the porter on duty. Tom had addressed it himself. He had written Simon's name and the name of the college on the front. Then in the top right corner he had written "Personal and Confidential, by hand to addressee". All very neat and clear. I had to explain to the porter that he was to deliver it by hand to Simon only, and not under any circumstances to any third party. Tom made me repeat the instructions more than once. As if he didn't really trust me but for some reason he couldn't go himself.'

'You say you didn't know what was in it. But I assume he didn't put stuff in his own envelopes. You did all that for him.'

'Usually, yes. But not this time. I never knew what was inside. He asked me to get two of those special envelopes. A4 size, with cardboard reinforcement. The sort they use for photographs.'

Photographs.

'Mr Harris? Your attention is wandering again. I said it was the sort of envelope they use for photographs. So they don't bend. Whatever it was he put in it I never saw it. Might have been photographs. I never asked. It was nothing to do with me. He sealed it himself, all around. I suppose he thought I might want to peep inside. I couldn't have cared less.'

'And the second envelope?'

'The same size and weight exactly.'

'Which college? Who was the addressee?'

'St Cuthbert's. I can't remember the name on the envelope. Exactly the same instructions.'

'And when was this?'

'A couple of days after Simon was found dead. Look, as I said, if you've got anything on him then good luck to you. My loyalty these days is to just one person. That's me. So go ahead. Just do me a favour and get him before he drinks himself to death.'

'I'm sorry, Sheila, I have a couple more questions. Then I'll leave you in peace. Does... did your firm use private detectives?'

She shook her head. 'No. We did commercial stuff, mostly. No divorces or anything like that.'

'But Tom would have known how to find one?'

'Oh yes. Criminal lawyers use them all the time and he knew plenty of those. A word in the right ear would have done the trick.'

'Was Tom in the office round about the last week in May of last year? That would have been between your two deliveries.'

She grinned, emptily, a distant look in her eyes. I had lost her attention. I would get no more answers. Unwilling to give up so soon I repeated my question verbatim. This time she focussed her eyes on me, frowning slightly. Perhaps it was not too late.

'You know,' she said, very slowly after a long pause, 'you'd have made a fucking good barrister. A real terrier. Why the hell didn't you go in for law? You'd have made a bomb, never mind all that modest salary rubbish. All right, my learned friend. I think he did have some time off about then. He went to the cottage for a few days. It hadn't been sold by then, though the chill winds were beginning to blow. Said he had to unwind. Too much stress. I had strict instructions not to try to contact him. He said he would cut off the phone. Fact is, he was unwinding every day, here in this very bar, so God knows why he needed to go there to unwind. But I didn't ask any questions. I held everything together in his absence, as I always did. I can't remember the exact dates he was away. He was back by the time the news came through about his brother. Then he went straight off to see his parents. You can get the dates from the appointments diary. It's on the floor by the coffee mug. Big square thing, hard blue cover. Most of it empty the last few months.'

'Last question, I promise. Can you give me the name and address of the barge?'

She pursed her lips. 'There's no address as such. Just a mooring spot on the canal. I'll draw you a diagram. It's quite easy to find. If you're thinking of going there, though, I'd take some muscle with you. Unless you go when he's had a few too many. Even then he can be dangerous. I know. I still have the bruises to prove it. I'd show you but they're in rather intimate places and I'd prefer not to undress in public. Is that it?'

'That's it. I'll get back to your office, or what's left of it, and have a look through his brother's stuff now. You can stay here if you like. I can find my own way. Have another drink on me. I'm sorry it's been so awful for you. I hope you get a new job soon. You're well qualified and experienced. And very resourceful.'

'Yes, I'm experienced all right. At covering for a fraud. He could yet go to prison, you know. And that's without anything you might have on him. And who's going to want to take on someone they'll see as his accomplice? No, I'm a *persona non grata* around here. That's Latin, isn't it? I've typed a lot of Latin words for him over the years. Usually I had no idea what they meant. But I know what that means. Maybe someone will take me on as a filing clerk somewhere. Or I could change profession. How about nursing assistant in an old people's home? I'm good at clearing up shit.'

I gave her a five-pound note in return for the slip of paper on which she had drawn her crude map of where I could find the barge. I watched as she lurched up to the bar, waving the money. Then I slipped quietly out.

TWENTY-EIGHT

A few minutes later I was back in the dusty shell of what had been your brother's office, staring at the boxes containing your things. But the image revolving in my mind was in Oxford, back in that summer. At the spot where your punt had been found, a young couple had moored theirs while the man tried to cool a bottle of champagne in the water. He had leaned far out of the punt, in danger of falling in. No, not really. No danger. Hard to capsize a punt. To fall into the water from a punt in that position, you had to get most of your body weight outside. It would take considerable physical effort. I had seen that for myself, in the actions of that silly couple who had dared to desecrate that holy spot. Seen but not understood. Looked with the eyes of the blind.

I found the appointments book. It was on the floor, where she had said. On the day you died he was away. In Suffolk, supposedly. Uncontactable.

At our first meeting Tom had asked me what I had found

in the boxes. Books, essays, records, clothes, I had told him, as well as a folder with his personal papers. Anything else? he had asked.

The photographs? Surely you would have destroyed your copies. Alban and I always assumed that. Tom would have thought the same. But were we right? Was there another way of looking at this?

Come on, Simon, help me see this through your eyes. Yes, they were taken and sent to you with an evil purpose. But what they showed was not evil. It was a record of your love. You never intended to have such a record. But might at least part of you have wanted to keep them, to hold them against a future when things would be different, when they would not pose any danger? And while you were deciding, what would you do with them? You would hide them. But nothing was found. Tom had had the boxes here for over a year and found nothing. Books, essays, records, clothes. All the detritus of an undergraduate life cut short before its term.

Records. Vinyl long-playing records with jackets and sleeves. I held my breath. At the time I had not thought to look inside them, but I did not know then what I was looking for. Tom did. But he was always in a hurry. Would it have occurred to him to search thoroughly for something he did not expect to find? What else might Tom have been concerned about? How did he arrange the meeting? There were no phones in the student rooms. Letter? Sheila had not been asked to deliver a letter. A note inside the envelope containing the photographs?

I took the sleeves out carefully, one by one, and laid them on the floor. With each one I then ran my hand around the inside of the empty cover, in case the note had been separated from the photographs. The fifth cover looked bulkier than the others. *The Times They Are a-Changin'.* Bob Dylan. That could have been your anthem, Simon, couldn't it? Times changing but not fast enough for you and Alban. Was that why you chose that one?

The envelope was inside. The photographs, identical to those I had destroyed. Something else. Two pieces of paper. A handwritten note and a map, with a spot marked in red ink.

You didn't leave a note. Why should you? You never expected to die. But you did leave a trail. Have you been trying all this time to lead me here, despairing at my slowness and my stupidity?

TWENTY-NINE

The two great concrete gashes of the Westway above me cast shadows onto the towpath in the early evening sunlight. Invisible traffic whooshed and swished.

I found the *Aurora* a few yards further on, exactly where Sheila had shown me. It was bus-length, squatting low in the turgid water which lapped sulkily against the side. The sloping faces of the enclosed upper section were painted a sickly green, with four square windows blanked out by blinds. On a tiny deck at one end, with barely room for anyone standing on it to turn around, stood a bright red Calor gas cylinder by a waist-high, knees-wide metal door leading into the enclosure, and a crate of empty beer bottles. At the stern was a rusty S-shaped tiller. The top of the enclosure was adorned with several withered plants in rusting buckets, an upturned wheelbarrow and a single bent bicycle wheel. I wondered how long it had been since the vessel had last chugged along the waterways. Did it even have a working engine? The whole gave the impression of a gigantic water-beetle hooked permanently to the bank and unable or unwilling to break free. No wonder its owner had been content to let Tom take possession. Neglect had surely placed it beyond the prospect of sale or repair.

The metal door of the barge swung open and Tom emerged. He threw an empty bottle down onto the deck, where it shattered noisily. He looked up, peering and shaking his head. I stepped forward. He wore loosely tied spotted pyjamas under an open grey flannel dressing gown, and oversized slippers which hung at the end of his feet. From his direction came a smell of stale beer, wine, tobacco and… yes, urine. I imagined what the stench would be like in the enclosed interior.

'Who the fuck is that? Oh it's you, Professor.'

He growled rather than spoke the words but they were still clear enough. He had just disposed of one bottle but had yet to start on the evening's serious drinking. I had to remember Sheila's warning. Even when drunk he was still dangerous.

'I'm just plain mister, you know. I told you that.'

'So what brings you down here? Well, as you are here, why not come aboard? It's not exactly a luxury yacht but it's kind of cosy. It does me. I suppose it was that cow Sheila who told you where I am.'

'That cow, as you call her, was loyal to you for far too long.'

'Her choice. More fool her. So why are you here?'

'I wondered if we could have a little chat. That's all.'

I stepped carefully onto the deck and, clenching my nostrils, followed him inside. It was as dank and reeking as I had feared. I fought hard against the impulse to throw up. Slowly my eyes adjusted to the gloom. There were crates of beer bottles at the far end in front of another tiny door. Along the two sides ran banquettes with torn plastic covers and protruding stuffing. Nothing else. I assumed there would be a kitchenette and toilet beyond the other door.

'So, welcome to my humble abode. Come on in and sit down. Have a beer.'

I sat down as close to the door as possible, noting to my relief that he had not secured the latch.

'No thanks.'

'Mind if I do?'

'Of course not. It's your place.'

'Well, it's not, actually. I suppose Sheila told you that as well. Belongs to a mate of mine.'

'Yes, she told me that.'

'I suppose she also told you I'm retired.'

'Yes. Forcibly retired.'

He took out a bottle from one of the crates and came back to sit opposite me. He grasped the bottle so hard I thought it would break. Then in a single, well-practised move he picked up an opener from the floor and flicked off the top of the bottle. He took a long draught and wiped his mouth again.

'Christ, is there anything that bloody woman didn't tell you?'

'Only that you owe her rather a lot of money. Not only her.'

He grunted. 'She's welcome to take anything I've got. Which is precisely nothing. Not this place, nothing inside it, not even what I'm drinking. So, go on, let's hear it. What have you got to say?'

He leaned back and stared at the low ceiling with its single dim light bulb. I had rehearsed my words, to be delivered like a verdict on a poor essay.

'You were in the punt with him when your brother died. You killed him.'

I expected anger, disbelief, shock. Not the manic laughter which seemed to erupt from above and around him and continued for half a minute.

'And it's taken you all this time to work that out,' he said, when he had recovered his breath. 'You know, my dear prof, I think you are suffering from a severe emotional deficit. You pry into the lives of others because you have no proper life yourself.'

'Yes, Tom, you're right. Can I call you Tom? I plead guilty to that. Only this is actually the first time I have ever pried into anyone else's life, as you put it. I always kept my distance from people. Even my students. I taught them and that was all. They passed through my rooms and on to their futures, taking with them some of the knowledge I gave them and the patterns of thought I tried to bring out in them. It was like that for years. Until one of them killed himself. Or so it was thought. And I wondered why I had suspected nothing about his intentions. So I began to ask myself why not. I began to look into aspects of his life I should have asked about while he was still alive. And I didn't like what I found. I didn't like the way his family reacted to his death. So I wondered about that. And I started to look into myself.'

'And did you like what you found? In yourself, I mean?'

'No.'

'Because you realised you were just an empty shell. And you were looking to fill it by sticking your fingers into the lives of other people, people who had suffered a tragic loss of the sort you can have no idea about because you have no family, just at the time they were trying to come to terms with it. Don't you think you should find some other way of coping with your inadequacies, Professor, and leave people to cope in their own way? And if you disapprove of that way, could I politely suggest that it is really none of your fucking business.'

'I think there's some truth in all that, Tom, and I did not like myself for it. But what I mainly didn't like was the way I had walled myself off. I had never faced up to that until this business forced me to.'

'Yes, that's really sad. My heart bleeds for you. So you think coming down here with all this nonsense is the way to put that right, to get out from behind that wall. What a tedious, pointless life you must have been leading. What was your field, did you say? Ancient literature or something like that? That must really set the blood racing, I don't think. Then one day, right out of the blue, up pops a nice little real-life mystery and you just can't let it go. You can't bear the thought of going back to your boring routine in your ivory tower. But maybe the thought you really can't bear is that your mystery is really no mystery at all. We all know what happened. Including you. So why not have a drink, and just let it go?'

He moved his eyes down until they met mine. He must have seen that he had hit home with some painful truths. There was still no suggestion of violence in his demeanour. He had used different weapons, ones whose effectiveness he knew all too well. He might have been a shadow of what he once was but he was not yet defenceless.

'Oh, I intend to let it go. Only just not yet. You see, it's not about putting myself right. It's about me finding myself in a position I had never sought. You are right about that. And believe me, after tonight, I will certainly be going back to what you call my ivory tower.'

He grinned. 'But you'll be missing us, won't you, even though you can't stand us? So, what's that position you never sought? Speaking up for Simon, now he's gone?'

'Yes, I suppose you could put it like that.'

'All right. I suppose I can't get rid of you until you have your say. So, go on with your story.'

'I know where the whisky and pills came from. Your parents' house. Your father's whisky and your mother's pills.'

He nodded. 'Yes, he took them from there. That's obvious. Is that it? Unless you're accusing them as well.'

'Maybe. I'm not sure what part they played, your father at any rate. But you're the one who was in the punt with him.'

'Really? I don't know one end of a punt from the other, not having had the privilege of being to your esteemed university. But I'm sorry for interrupting. Please do go on. It's been a long time since anyone read me a goodnight fairy tale.'

'You met him at a pre-arranged point. He moored the punt there. You had sent him copies of incriminating photographs. You had the negatives with you. The deal was that he drank the whisky and took the pills while you destroyed the negatives, bit by bit. I must admit, the punt was a brilliant idea. Anybody seeing you would have assumed you were just a couple of students larking about. Even by the time he was in a really bad way they would only have seen a young lad drinking too much and looking the worse for wear. In the end he was too far gone to resist. That was when you toppled him into the water. You see, in the state he was in he could not have got into the water on his own. He needed help.'

He shrugged his shoulders and spat onto the floor.

'Is that it, Professor? The whole story? Yes, it's interesting. Interesting, I mean, that neither the police nor the coroner were prepared to see it that way. Because it was so fucking obvious he intended to kill himself. That was why he took the whisky and pills with him.'

'No. You brought those. So it would look like suicide.'

A sneer formed on his face. 'What do they call that place you come from? The city of dreaming spires. I'd call it the place of spiralling dreams. Hey, that's not bad, is it? Fantasies. Lost causes. Like you and your theories. And your imaginary photographs. You have no evidence. No proof. You've brought nothing with you. So I suggest that now you've had your fun you get the fuck out of here now and never come back. Sorry not to put it more politely.'

'Yes, I promise you that. I will never come here again. But as I am here, perhaps you could tell me something. Get some things off your chest. It's good for you, so they say. We're alone here. So tell me. Why?'

'Why did I kill him? I've already told you. I didn't. I wasn't there.'

'No, I mean, why this? Why here, drinking yourself to death? Because that is what you're doing, isn't it? Why give up all you had and all you were? You were good at your job, Sheila told me. Now you've nothing. Even this barge isn't yours.'

'Yes, very clever. I can see where you're going with this. You've convinced yourself I killed him and now I'm plagued by a guilty conscience. So I've taken to drink in a big way, so much so that I couldn't keep my business afloat. Well, you're wrong about that. Because this has been going on for a long time. I don't mind telling you about it. Perhaps it's about time people like you realised how people like me live, in the real world. It takes years to build up the sort of thing I had. The business, the trust of the clients, the properties. And when the end comes it doesn't just happen overnight. One client is paid a little late so decides to move on. He tells others who also back off. It's all right at first, because the bank trusts you and makes further loans. After all, it was the bank who took a chance on you in the first place and set you up and they trust their own judgement. So you stay afloat, just. You wait for the tide to turn. You wait for better times, for that one big contract that will refloat the whole boat, that big deal about which the word gets around the whole village – because it is a village, the legal world of London – and sends your ratings soaring up again, so that soon you have far more work than you can handle, so you take on more staff, lease a bigger office, invest in more properties, plan your retirement in your forties with a yacht and a big house in the country and cottage in the Dordogne. Yes, I had it all worked out. But it didn't happen. The new clients didn't come. The loyal ones stayed loyal for a while, until they too found their claims delayed and their payments not made. And they spread the word because their world is part of that same village. But still the loans came in. But now they wanted repaying, sooner and in bigger chunks. So the securities had to be sold. The properties, the investments. It's a vicious circle. I could have got out of it sooner. Before it all got out of control. Why didn't I? Because they would never have understood. My parents, I mean. All their lives they had been counting on me. So what would have happened if I had gone home to visit without the sports car? If I had to tell them their place in Spain had gone? So I kept up the charade. Borrowed that car I was in when I went up to your place to pick up his things. It was ludicrous. Like you're holding up a building with no foundation. You're running around propping up this bit here, and that bit there, and the bit you're not propping up at the moment is where it starts to crumble because you can't be everywhere at once. And all you're doing is making sure the whole thing comes crashing down all the sooner. Christ, I need another beer.'

I waited until he had fetched the bottle and returned to his seat. He opened it, this time with a little less panache than before.

'So if your parents had gone out to Spain this year?'

'They wouldn't. She hasn't been well enough for some time. I kept that place until last. Just in case she made a miraculous recovery.'

'There are no miracles with her condition. Soon she won't know who you are.'

'You know, that's a bloody great relief. No questions about how well things are going, no need for the endless lies, the false reassurances, the cheerfulness put on like a coat against the storm of reality. That's all so bloody exhausting.'

'But he isn't losing his memory. And he will have to know sooner or later.'

'He'll know eventually. Why spoil his illusions before then? And with her mind gone, he won't be too bothered. It was her he was always concerned about. She needed my success. He needed it because she needed it. Without her, maybe we'll be able to be just like a normal father and son. I'll go up there and live with him, after she's gone. Get some sort of job. He'll carry on until he gets his pension. We won't have much but it will be enough. Go out to the pub once a week. Go to the football once a week. That's what normal people do, don't they? That's how they live. I've never been to a football match, you know. It's not a bad idea, is it, to plan to have a normal life like that, just the two of us? You know, my dearest prof, I feel happier now than for years. Now I have nothing at all. No responsibilities. I own nothing. My time is my own. No phone calls, no worried clients pestering me with their ridiculous little problems, no late-night reading of case notes, no money worries. No point worrying about something you don't have. Yes, me and my dad. We'll settle down together. After she's gone. I wouldn't want him to be left on his own.'

His speech was now a little slurred but still clear enough. As he spoke about his dream, he looked upwards, his eyes moistening. How often, here in the quiet of his water-borne prison, had he consoled himself with that very dream, waiting for the mists of inebriation to obscure the reality which would always remind him it could never be?

'Yes, Tom, it's a nice thought, to live like that. Without her to disturb you. And without him. You know who I mean. Just the two of you. You and your dad, enjoying a quiet life together. Only it can't be, can it?'

'Why not?'

'You know you can't escape. There won't ever be just the two of you, will there? There will be a ghost spoiling your little scene of domestic bliss. He's here now. If he wasn't, you wouldn't be down here, would you? You'd be up there already, with both your parents, having honestly admitted your failures, which your father would have forgiven because he would have had no choice, looking after her, helping him, planning that future you just talked about. But you won't and you can't. Because you'd be taking that ghost with you, the one that will destroy all the remains of your hopes and his. So you have to stay here until the end, keeping the ghost captive here, to protect him. The two of you haven't seen each other since you plotted it and he gave you the bottles, have you? And you never will. That's the truth, isn't it? You couldn't bear to see each other, to be reminded of what you did, to realise in the expressions on your faces that you know it was all in vain, that you destroyed an innocent young life for no reason.'

He looked down again. When he spoke at last it was almost in a whisper.

'Fuck off, Professor. Get out. Get out or I'll throw you out.'

'All right, I'm going. Thank you for your hospitality. And the chat.'

I rose and opened the door.

THIRTY

A bulky figure stood in the doorway as I opened it. I stepped back to allow it to enter. Tom sprang out of his seat and went for the door, stumbling as he failed to get enough purchase on the floor from his loose slippers. The newcomer grabbed his arms and pushed him back in. Another, slighter figure emerged from the deck and stepped quietly into the room. I closed the door behind us. Tom was lying on the floor.

'You bastard!' he growled between clenched teeth. 'You cowardly bastard. There was me thinking you were being brave or foolhardy, however you want to look at it. And all along you had a fucking bodyguard.'

I sat down again.

'Tom, let me introduce Major Maximilian Harding. He was until very recently in the army in a special service unit. He's trained in all the martial arts and he can break your back in three places with one arm while holding the other behind his back and singing "Danny Boy". You may not believe all of that but I seriously recommend that you do not try to find out what he is capable of. And I believe you know Alban Knight. Knight as in of the Round Table. Simon's friend. Not know him in the flesh, of course. But you've seen photographs of him, very much in the flesh.'

Max was standing in front of the door, smiling. Nobody familiar only with the formally dressed upright figure who presided over the lodge of our college would have recognised him. He wore a thick bomber jacket with a close-fitting hood, leather trousers and heavy boots. Alban was wearing the open black leather coat he had on when I first met him, over the same blue jeans and loose pullover. He was carrying a briefcase, which he handed to me. I made room for him to sit beside me. Max remained in position, barring Tom's exit. I ran my hand across the handle of the case and down towards the clasp.

'So that's it,' said Tom. 'You want a confession. And if I don't give it willingly this heavy here gets to beat it out of me. I'm sure he'd enjoy that. And I suppose that queer young creep over there gets to write it all down. So what do you think a confession like that is worth? And you still haven't said why you think I did it.'

'I'm waiting for you to tell me why you did it. I don't need anyone to beat it out of you. Max is only here in case you decide to take out your frustrations on me, the way you used to take them out on Sheila. Yes, she told me about that.'

'She's a lying bitch.'

'I don't think so. Was she lying when she told me about the trips you told her to make to Oxford to deliver the photographs? One set to your brother and the other to his friend? Special delivery, by hand to addressee only.'

He struggled to sit upright. 'Photographs! Here you go again. Still going on about photographs. What bloody photographs?'

'I have evidence for what I'm saying. I know you'll say it would never stand up in court and I'm sure you'd be right. But it's enough for me.'

'What? Her word that she went to Oxford to deliver a couple of envelopes? Evidence? Give me a break.'

'When you first came to see me, to collect Simon's things, you asked me if I had found anything else, apart from the usual stuff I had told you about. What were you thinking of?'

I looked pointedly down at the case and again fingered the clasp.

'All right. She did deliver some envelopes for me. She delivered lots of things I couldn't trust to the post. She never knew what was in them. You've got it into your head that there were incriminating photographs inside, whatever that means. And now you're pretending you've got something in that case which incriminates me. Well, if you have, show me. And I'll tell you what it's worth. As if you didn't know already.'

'I think you know what I've got here. I saw them. The ones you sent to Alban here, at St Cuthbert's. He entrusted them to me.'

'So where are they now?'

'I destroyed them. That was what Alban wanted. Didn't you, Alban?'

Alban nodded. From the moment he had sat down beside me, he had fixed Tom with a steady stare, betraying no emotion in his face. He continued to stare as Tom rose unsteadily and found his way back to his seat. Tom avoided Alban's eyes while he fixed his on mine, glancing occasionally down at the briefcase. We sat in silence for a minute while I waited for the question I knew would follow. When Tom spoke at last his voice was quiet, empty of expression.

'So if you destroyed them, where's your evidence now?'

'They weren't the only copies, as you know. You also sent them to Simon. You thought they might still be with his things. But more likely he had destroyed them. I thought the same, when I found out about them. So you looked through the boxes as soon as you got them back to the office. But you're not a patient man, are you? No time to go looking through all those record covers.'

He shook his head and sighed.

'Record covers? So that's… No. I'm not a patient man. You're right about that. But I can still think. And if you think I'm going to say a single word more with that thug in here you're seriously mistaken.'

I turned to Max. 'It's all right. You can leave us now. I'll see you later in that pub on the corner.'

'Are you sure, Mr Harris?'

'Oh, it speaks, does it?' muttered Tom.

'Careful,' I said. 'Remember what I said about his skill in the martial arts. Yes, Max, I'm sure.'

Max smiled beatifically at the three of us, clicked his heels, opened the door and stepped onto the deck. Alban maintained his gaze and his silence while I continued to hold onto the case, stroking the leather exterior from time to time. We could have been three strangers in a station waiting room, careful to avoid inappropriate verbal contact. After a few minutes Tom coughed and sat upright. I had the impression he was trying to remember how he would have addressed an opposing solicitor.

'You do realise there's still no proof, even if you have got them there? Just in case you were thinking of going to the police.'

'We know that. Even though we also have your letter and the map. We're not going to the police. We're going to destroy them all. Tell you what. Let's play a little game. I'll destroy these now. Tear them up, bit by bit, and throw them in the water. So you'll know they're gone. Just like you did with him.'

I opened the case and took out the envelope.

'You said you won't come back. But he might.'

'Who?'

'Him. The queer sitting next to you. The one who's taken a vow of silence but who keeps staring at me.'

'Alban's half your size. And he wouldn't hurt a fly.'

'He might come with that gorilla.'

'You beat up your girlfriend, when that was what she was supposed to be. Now you're afraid of a student and our head porter. I'm not surprised you're a coward. The way you killed him was cowardly. That's all you are. A bully and a coward. Nobody will come. You have my word. I can speak for the three of us.'

'Head porter? You said—'

'Max is our head porter. You must have missed him when you visited the college. He was in the army. I wasn't lying about that. Perhaps it was a bit of an exaggeration to say he could break your back in three places. No, he won't come. This ends tonight.'

He looked down, wringing his hands. 'Yes. Yes. That's right. It ends tonight. All right. What do you want to know?'

'When did you find out Simon was homosexual?'

'I didn't.'

'You're lying. Come on. Stop playing stupid games. You had these photographs taken to show him you knew. So you must have realised beforehand, or at least suspected. But you weren't living at home during what we can call Simon's developmental years. You wouldn't have noticed. So who told you? Was it your father?'

He glared at me, at last summoning signs of the anger he had buried for so long. 'You're determined to bring him into this, aren't you? It started a couple of years before... before Simon died. My father would drop hints. Things he'd noticed about Simon's behaviour. That he didn't seem interested in girls. Then he, my father, would have much longer conversations with me about it. Tell me how disgusted he was at the very thought. Disgusted with himself, as well. That he could have fathered someone like that. Or maybe it was the way his mother had brought Simon up. She had been too great an influence on him. She had feminised him. It was his own fault as well, he said, because he had not been a countervailing influence. He had not shown Simon how to be a man in the modern world. He went on and on like that. I didn't want to hear it. I mean, I don't like queers. But frankly, I couldn't be bothered who does what in their private lives. I had enough on my plate. I couldn't care less what Simon got up to. But the old man was getting obsessed. Before that, he would talk to me about my work and I would tell him how great things were and that was how we got by. It was a sort of ritual and we were both comfortable with it. Even when I knew things were beginning to go pear-shaped. But now he was going on about something which was nothing to do with me or my business. Something I couldn't give a damn about. Until he started to go on about how it would affect her, tip her over the edge.

'It started as a sort of joke at first. Between me and the old man. The idea that somehow Simon might do away with himself and solve the problem that way. What would be the best way? Some people took pills. Like the ones she had. We were alone, in the hall, when he first mentioned the pills. I had been up there on a short visit and was on my way out to the car. She was out the back, drying dishes. She liked to do that. She'd already started taking clean ones out of the cupboard to wash and dry them all over again. She couldn't have heard or seen us. I tried to make a joke out of it, the way we usually did. Then I realised he was serious. I lost it. I took him by the throat. I was sick with anger. After all I had already done for them, getting them out of the financial mess they had got themselves into, making it possible for them to have nice things and go on holidays abroad, when once all that had seemed impossible. I had given them back their lives. And now this. All right, I said at last, I'll fix it. This one last thing. Then it will be over between us, I told him. No more obligations either way. We'll be finished. I've spent my whole life fixing things for the two of you and I'll fix this. I'll put someone onto it, to make some enquiries. There may be nothing in it, nothing to worry about. If there is, I'll sort it. And that will be the end. You and I are done. That's what I told him. Yes, you are right, Professor. That future, with the pub and the football, just the two of us after she had gone, that was never going to be. That was all over long ago. I hired a private detective. What he came up with confirmed our worst fears. But it also put a tool into my hands. Simon's friend, as you called him. His fellow queer over there next to you. Now I had something I could use. That, and the photos. I told the old man to get hold of the bottles. I even thought about fingerprints. I made sure I never touched the bottles.'

'You told your father you would sort it. Did you always mean to kill him?'

He shook his head violently. 'I never planned to kill him. That's the truth. I would tell the old man afterwards that it had only been necessary to push him to the brink. But I didn't know I was playing with fire. I'm a lawyer, not a fucking biochemist. It went all right at first. He knew the deal. Simon, I mean. The whisky and pills to see the negatives destroyed, bit by bit. He was chatty, at the beginning. Told me he had met someone, another guy, how much in love they were, how they had planned to be open about their affair. Now he understood he would need to be discreet. He promised. Swore. Was that not enough for me? I had made my point. "Come on," he said, "just throw the rest of them in the water and let me go back. You can go back to London and we'll forget all about it." "Not just yet," I said. "Take some more, and I'll throw away some more. It's just a game," I said, "let's play some more." He seemed fine. Too fine. Not afraid enough. I needed for him to be afraid, you see. Really afraid. I needed for him to look death in the eye. Otherwise I could not trust his promises. I could not take them back to my father and reassure him he was safe.'

I was aware that Alban was shaking. I glanced sideways at him. There were tears on his cheeks. Yet he maintained the stillness and the silence he had promised at that midnight conference in my room when I had told him and Max what I had found and we had decided what to do next, that we would confront him together, that I would go in first to prepare the ground while they waited outside, that I would do the talking while their presence would feed his fear and perhaps, just perhaps, his conscience.

'It happened very suddenly,' he continued. 'One moment he was still chatting, though his speech was a bit disconnected by then. But only the way it would have been if he had just been a bit drunk. The next moment, his eyes were rolling and he couldn't get his breath. His hand was at his throat. There was this horrible rattling sound. Then he went quiet. Still and quiet. I panicked. I was sure he had died. A heart attack or something. Maybe he was not as strong as I thought. Maybe his heart was naturally weak. I looked around. Nobody there. The last movement he had made was to turn to the side of the punt. So he was already part way out. It was easy to get my hands underneath. The side of the punt dipped with his weight. He just slid in, barely a sound. Not until just before he hit the water. Then there was a little moan. Some sort of reflex, I suppose. There was no sign of physical resistance. No sign that he was waking up. I watched to see if he would regain consciousness and fight his way out. He didn't. I closed my eyes. When I opened them he was gone. I left the bottles where they were. I threw the rest of the negatives into the water. I walked off. That's all.'

'And was it worth it? She was already losing her memory. Simon could have told her everything and she'd have had difficulty remembering who he even was, never mind what he was up to in his love life. And you said yourself, this whole business finished everything between you and your father. You did it to save them. When you did it before, they revered you. But that was only about money and what it could buy for them. Now you had gone far beyond that. You had killed for them. And they are strangers to you. And here you are. Yes, I hope it was worth it.'

I stood up, helping Alban to his feet. Tom looked up.

'Oh, are you going? You're not going to stay and have a nightcap. What about one for the road? No? Okay. Goodbye, little queer. Goodbye, Professor. It has been nice talking to you. I'm sorry if I was a bit hostile at times. Actually, I like you and respect you. You're a good man. He was lucky to have you as his tutor. Yes, very lucky...'

THIRTY-ONE

So, Simon, it all started with your father, a man to whom I had taken an instant and, at the time, inexplicable dislike. What was it Molly had told me about him? He always seemed to have a suit of armour on. He never had time for you. Hated all that business about church and music. Regarded them as weaknesses, tolerable in a woman but not in a man. He was a man in control of himself and his feelings.

But when he knew about you he was no longer in control. He called on Tom to fix the problem. He provided Tom with the means, knowing what the outcome might be.

What were the warning signs he noticed? There could be many. An accidental mannerism, a certain way of speaking, a spontaneous reaction to a photograph or image or story on television or radio. Then maybe something more telling. No apparent interest in the opposite sex, increasingly suspicious as the years went by. Why were they so important to him? What if he was not after all a different sort of man from you, but one all too similar, the only real difference being your honesty? Maybe he was just like you at your age, loving the same things, being sensitive in the same ways. Hating then what he saw in himself, how could he fail to hate it again when it re-emerged in you? How could he tolerate a son who was the opposite of all he now believed in, whose eyes were already looking to a future which would make a mockery of the life he had chosen for himself? It was not to be borne.

But what, then, about your mother? Maybe I was wrong. It did not all start with your father but with her. What did she really know, that time I visited her? Even if words and memories were eluding her, that did not mean she had no more understanding. Her expression as she stood at the door as I was leaving spoke of a grief all the more agonising for being beyond expression. You and she had been close, in a manner of speaking, when she had been able to bask in your musical talent and your piety.

Then she lost you. All mothers lose their sons when they grow up. But she lost you in another, much more painful way. She could not articulate her betrayal or act on it. But your brother could. He could act for your father and himself to protect your mother from a revelation which could spell the end of what was left of her sanity. They could not take the risk of thinking that she was beyond anything you could do to her.

I have never understood families, Simon. Maybe what I have told you of my own story will help to explain that. But I was beginning to understand yours a little. Only beginning. Much was still unclear. What was clear was that theirs was a marriage of convenience, for both of them. If I was right about his suppressed nature, marriage and children were an important safeguard, one which many such men chose in those times. As for her reasons for choosing him, I was still in the dark. He offered neither attraction nor ambition. After the failure of their short-lived business venture her ambitions passed to your brother. It was his job to provide the material goods she needed. Tom accepted that because it brought what he had never known up to then, their approval and admiration. He became addicted to the worship and gratitude they offered him and to seeing them find some sort of balance in their lives. She at last had the trappings for which she had longed. Your father had less resentment to bear. It was precarious but better than before.

But you too had a role to play. In a way, Tom's was the easier. Yours only became clear when you grew up. When you were young, your mother found out how to live through you, through your going to church and being an altar boy, then through your music. Later, she wanted you for something different. Something her husband had never been able to provide. Something she had never wanted him to provide. Affairs were out of the question, forbidden by the God who still ruled her inner life, whose finger pointed accusingly at her even for passing thoughts of impurity. Or was there another reason, a deep-seated revulsion, a fear of memories that the touch or even the look of another man might recall? So she turned to you. No fear there, no revulsion. Just the natural pride of a mother at seeing her son grow up. Innocent and natural.

Except that it was neither. She did not realise, not until it was too late, the far greater impurity of the looks she turned on you than of those she might, if she had been a different woman, have turned on a friend or neighbour or passing stranger. What she did could only repel you and thus inflict the pain of rejection on her. You were only trying to create a natural distance between you and her. And as your own nature became clear to you, you were preparing to reject her in a way which would have destroyed her. So you had to be destroyed first.

But did you still have the power? Was she already living in her own world by then? Who could say what she could or could not remember?

Nobody had spoken up for you to her. Your father and brother were your judge, jury and executioner, and you had no presence at your trial. The dead have a right to have someone speak for them. It would not matter if she did not understand and could say nothing in return. If there was anything left in her mind for me to reach I needed to try.

First, I would write to Molly. I needed her help. And she was entitled to know all I now knew.

THIRTY-TWO

Molly opened the door and stepped outside, leaving it half open. She was carrying an empty shopping bag.

'She's calm today,' she whispered, 'but I doubt if she will respond very much, if at all. I'll leave you to it. I did say you were coming, but I don't think it sank in. So you will have to remind her who you are. I'll be off now. I'll give you a full hour. There's a pot of tea in there, still fresh, and an extra cup. Help yourself. And remember… be as gentle as you can.'

She touched my arm and moved slowly down the front path and onto the pavement. She glanced back once, an anxious look on her face, but did not stop. I stepped inside.

Your mother was sitting on the sofa, as before. And as before, she did not look up, remaining motionless. I sat down and poured myself a cup of tea. To my surprise my hands did not shake.

'Hello, Mrs Harvey. Your sister very kindly let me in. She's gone to the shops. Well, you know that, don't you? Because she told you.'

The same little brown bottle of pills on the table by the teapot.

'I don't know if you remember me,' I continued, casually. 'I have been here before. My name is Alan Harris. I was his tutor, at Oxford. I mean Simon's tutor. You remember he was there, at Oxford? He was doing very well. Until this awful thing happened. The reason I'm here is… I've brought some things of his for you. They were in his room. His room at college, I mean. Not his room here. Of course not. Why would I have anything from his room here? In any case, there's nothing there, is there? Your sister showed me last time. They belong to you now. These things. Not worth much, but they'll remind you of him. Not much here in the house to remember him by, is there? There was the piano but you got rid of that. Wanted the space, I suppose. For that sofa. Shall I show you what I've got? Look. There's his matriculation photo. Wearing his subfusc. That's what they call it. The outfit you have to wear for formal occasions. White bow tie, dark suit, gown, the works. He looks really grown-up, doesn't he? There he is, in the front row. See?'

I laid the photograph on the table in front of her and pointed to the image. She glanced down, then raised her head again. Still the same unfocussed stare, the same pursed lips.

'Oh, and here's a copy of the college magazine. Something there about a concert he was playing in. Of course you won't have heard him play. Not recently. Not since you got rid of the piano. No, before that. When he stopped playing for you. There's letters here, too. From a couple of his school friends. I suppose he lost touch with them after a while. That's what happens, when you make new friends. I couldn't find any of your letters to him. They must have got mislaid.'

I sat back in my chair and tried to draw her gaze. Her eyes were on me but it was impossible to tell what she saw. Her lips worked slightly. She swallowed. I waited, wondering if she was about to say something. Nothing.

'You do remember, don't you? I was told you might not. Something about you losing your memory. That's such a pity. So many wonderful memories about him, and you may not be able to hold on to them for much longer. Well, maybe these few things will help you. Because the last thing you want to lose are the memories of your child. I am right about that, aren't I? I mean, you would agree with me on that.'

She shifted a little in her chair. She turned her face towards the wall, her gaze moving from one flying duck to the other, as if wondering how they came to be there. It was time to move on, further and deeper.

'I know it was hard for you. When he left. Not left for college, I mean. Before that. When he stopped going to church for you. It was all for you, wasn't it? The priest told me. You couldn't bear to go to church yourself, not any more. So he went in your place. He said the prayers for you, took the sacraments for you. It didn't work, did it?'

She turned her head towards me. There was a visible trembling in her lips. I had struck home. Not only that. I had gone too far. Any minute now she would lose control, scream at me, throw me out, perhaps have a complete breakdown. But I was not ready to stop. I had much further to go, down into those treacherous waters where maybe both of us might drown.

'Then there was something else you wanted him to do for you, wasn't there, when he was older? When he grew tall and good-looking. But that didn't work either, did it? You repelled him, disgusted him. He rejected you. Broke your heart. Shall I get us some more tea?'

I rose and went through to the kitchen, carrying the tray. The interruption was not just to give her a chance for my words to take root, if they ever could. My initial calm was deceptive. I thought I was about to faint. The blood was pounding in my ears. I took deep breaths as I busied myself with the kettle, the cups and the milk jug. I surely had no cause to worry, I told myself. By the time I returned with the tea she would have forgotten what I had just said, or even that I was there. She had set up barriers in her mind to stop unwanted truths getting through from within. What chance did I have of reaching her from a far greater distance?

I returned to the sitting room, gripping the tray with great care. I sat down and began to pour the tea. Only then did I look up. Her expression was as fixed as it had been when I had first begun to speak to her.

'He wasn't just doing well in his work,' I said, placing a cup on the table in front of her. She ignored it. 'He had fallen in love, and it was mutual. Well, that happens with young people all the time, of course. It's only natural. But this was serious. Did he tell you? His brother knew but he won't have told you. Nor will your husband have mentioned it. You see, they thought it would upset you. I know he was planning to tell you himself, when the time was right. So I'll tell you now. I met him, you see. Got to know him quite well in fact.'

There was not the slightest flicker in the stern set of her features.

'Did you hear me, Mrs Harvey? Did you hear what I just said? I said that I met him. Do you want to know who I'm talking about? No, he didn't tell you and his brother didn't mention it. Obviously. So I'm telling you. Your son loved another man. So what do you think about that? There's rejection for you. You're out of his love life because you're his mother, and then even more out of it because it was a man took your place.'

I took a sip of tea before continuing. 'Oh dear! That's sad, isn't it? Because you wanted love as well, didn't you? Like everybody. Only for some reason it couldn't be for you the way it is for most people. Meeting someone in the normal course of your life, falling in love, getting married perhaps. You married, but not someone who could love you or whom you could love. Now, I know what you're going to say. Or rather what you would say if you were going to say anything. You'd say that what I just told you about him and his lover, that's not love either, that's a sickness, a perversion. At least you never had anything to do with that sort of thing. That's disgusting. That's what you'd say and you'd find quite a few people who would agree with you. Only I'm not one of them. Not after having known both of them. No, that was the real thing. That was real love, something you've never known. You should have been proud of him for that. You and your other son and your husband. Instead, you destroyed him.'

She was staring at me now. I held her gaze until one of us had to look away. At last she did so.

'Yes, that's what you did. All three of you. I accuse you all. They didn't tell you. But one day you would find out. And they couldn't bear the thought of what that would do to you. You had found a way, the three of you, to keep yourselves afloat on a sea of pretence and self-deception. But you only managed to do that by cutting him out of your lives. He was the danger, the hidden reef on which your delicately balanced little boat could founder. So you removed all traces of him from the house. Then you started to wipe him from your memories. So he never even existed. But there was always the danger that he would suddenly reappear and capsize you. That he would come crashing back into your life, bringing back with him all that pain of rejection, this time multiplied beyond endurance. Where would that have put you? It's too horrible even to think about. They could never have allowed that to happen. I mean your husband and your other son. Your protectors. Your barriers against reality. They had devoted their whole lives to keeping you safe from yourself. And to do that they had to keep you safe from him.

'So, your memory is going, is it? Maybe they're right about that. But I think you're aware of what is happening to you. I think you're controlling it, up to a point. You're a very controlling person, aren't you? I think you're deciding what memories will go first. You've already put him into a box marked gone. Less pain that way, less guilt. But I'm here to open that box again. I'm here to unpack those memories and hold them right here in front of your nose.'

I stood up and bent down so my eyes were less than an inch from hers. I whispered, 'I'm talking about the memories of your beautiful, sensitive son, of his voice, his music, his understanding, yes, his capacity for love, but not love for you because you felt nothing like love for him, his lost potential to grow up and become a man to bring many blessings to the world, all lost because you killed him. All those memories will be the last ones you lose, not the first.'

I returned to my chair.

'Yes, that's right,' I continued, now in a much louder voice than before. 'I accuse you, Mrs Harvey. You killed him. Your husband and his brother forced him to take his own life and that's killing, in my book. Your husband supplied the means, from this house. His brother was there with him when he died. He sat and watched him swallow a whole bottle of those pills of yours, swilling it down with whisky from your husband's cupboard here. Then, when Simon was on the point of losing consciousness, he tipped him into the water and watched him drown. I know. Tom told me. He confessed. Oh, don't be shocked. Be grateful. They did it for you. This all goes back to you. So why would you want to forget what they did for you? Oh no, you'll keep those memories and all the guilt that goes with them until every last cell of your memory has withered and died. And every time you try to put them back into that box before their time they'll just pop right back out again and hit you in the face. I'm not a religious man. But that's something I'm prepared to go down on my knees and pray for, every day.'

I heard a key turning in the front door lock. Molly returning. I rose, preparing to greet her with a smile. But the figure which loomed in the doorway was much bulkier than your aunt's slight frame. He stepped forward slowly. What had happened? He was home far too early. It was supposed to be his night for meeting his mates for a drink. Something he would never miss.

'Mr Harris,' he said. 'Nice of you to pop in.'

He put out his hand. I took it, my mind racing. Did he suspect why I was there? Had Tom overcome their estrangement and told him that in a moment of weakness he had confessed and implicated his father? Was this gesture of friendship the prelude to something violent? I was sure he was capable of it. I had no chance of getting past him and out through the front door. But surely he would not hit me in front of your mother. Where the hell was Molly?

'Well, this is a surprise, Mr Harris. I had no idea you were coming. You should have told me. We could have met at the pub for a drink.'

A smell of stale beer now pervaded the room. He was not drunk as far as I could tell, only displaying a rather more genial manner than at our previous meetings. But he still made no move to sit down. He still blocked my way to escape.

'Hello, Mr Harvey.' My voice sounded much too high-pitched to my ears. 'I just popped in to let you have some of Simon's things. You know, mementoes. Things to remember him by. I was just showing them to his mother. They're on the table there.'

'Yes, I know what mementoes are, thanks.'

For a moment I detected a note of menace in his voice. He shifted his weight from one foot to the other. Then the moment passed and the geniality returned.

'Still, it is a long way to come,' he said. 'Very thoughtful of you. So don't be rushing off now. Stay and have a drink.'

I glanced at your mother. She was staring blankly at the window. She seemed not to have noticed his entrance. He sat down at last, next to her. He rested his hand gently on her shoulder.

'That's very good of you. I really didn't want to impose.'

We were tiptoeing around each other, speaking only in clichés. The tension between us rose like a slow, silent tide.

'Normally,' I continued, 'this would be too early for me. But as you've been so kind, perhaps I could have a small whisky. Nothing special. Just what you would normally have if you were here on your own.'

He frowned slightly, then smiled again.

'Of course. Whisky it is. I'll join you. Just a little one. Doesn't do to mix beer and spirits too much.'

He rose and opened the drinks cupboard. Several bottles of cheap blend whisky were visible, alongside some small tumblers. He took out one of the bottles and two tumblers and started to pour.

'Just a very small one,' I called over to him.

He brought them over, placed mine on the table in front of me and sat down. He held his glass firmly in one hand, caressing your mother's arm with the other. That was for my benefit, to show me they were really a normal couple, grieving in their own undemonstrative way. I raised my glass towards my lips, stopping as soon as I caught a whiff of the pungent odour. I knew that if I brought it any nearer I would be sick. It reminded me of the paraffin we had used at home for the portable and extremely dangerous bathroom heater. Esso Blue. An overalled man in a little blue van came with deliveries every fortnight. For God's sake, don't let your mind wander! Keep alert.

'I see you have quite a stock over there, Mr Harvey. A favourite of yours, is it?'

He nodded. 'It does me. Can't really afford that single malt stuff. And to tell you the truth I couldn't tell the difference if you got me to do a blind tasting. So I'd be wasting my money.'

'I bet you wouldn't miss one of those bottles, if someone decided to help themselves when you weren't looking. Or maybe you keep a few so you can give one away from time to time. You know, just a little gift.'

What was I playing at? My situation was precarious enough as it was without my provoking him. But something was driving me on, making me lose control. He had filled his glass nearly to the brim, despite his declared intention only to have a small one. With a sudden movement he jerked his free arm upwards, opened his mouth and half emptied the glass into it. He swallowed hard and decisively. We stared at each other like tomcats meeting by chance in a garden, each holding his ground, testing the resolve of the other. He was strong but the effects of alcohol would slow him down. I was weak but quick, and I could be out of my chair and through the door before he could get to his feet.

'Yes,' I said at last, 'I see you like it. But money can't be a problem, can it? I mean, if you wanted to try some of the expensive stuff you could always ask Tom to send you a case or two. Money's no object to him, is it?'

His glare told me what he wanted me to know, that he might have betrayed himself but he would never break. He would never give me that satisfaction. His fingers dug tightly into your mother's arm but she showed no reaction.

'That's right, Mr Harris. Perhaps I will ask him. He's always ready to pay for little treats for us in our old age. Though as I said I doubt if I would taste any difference.'

'Have you been in touch lately? Have you rung him? Or has he rung you? Just wondering.'

'No, not lately. About time he rang us. He usually rings once a week at least. When he can manage it. Between all those cases he's handling. For his clients.'

'Of course. His important clients. But I'm sure he's thinking of you, even when he's too busy to ring. He told me he got you a place in Spain, for your holidays. That's so generous of him. Not many sons would do that for their parents. Not many would be in a position to. Whereabouts is it?'

'Near Marbella.' He pronounced the double Ls slowly and deliberately, twisting his lips into a sneer, telling me that he knew the correct pronunciation as well as I did but was not going to be so pretentious as to use it. 'Lovely place. Very secluded. Close to the beach but away from the crowds.'

'Sounds idyllic. Are you going there again this year?'

'Probably not. Not after the shock of all this business.' He could have been talking about a burglary, or a slight car accident. 'And as you can tell, my wife isn't really up to travelling at the moment.'

I sensed the immediate threat had receded. I stood up, still holding my glass at a safe distance.

'Well, I'd better be off, I suppose. Long way to go.'

He pointed to the glass. 'You haven't touched your drink.'

I looked at it as if I had not been aware of its existence until that moment.

'Oh, so I haven't. To tell you the truth, it makes me feel ill.' I turned towards her. 'I don't suppose you take whisky, do you,

Mrs Harvey? You wouldn't like to have a taste of this, would you? No, perhaps not. Very wise. Not on top of those pills. That could be very bad for you. The combination. Whisky and pills, I mean. Especially this whisky and those pills. Eh, Mr Harvey?'

I had moved towards the door and now stood between him and my escape route. He fluttered his fingers slightly, as if preparing to make a fist. A flicker of indecisive movement in his lips. His breathing a little faster and shallower. A flush in his cheeks.

'Well, it was very nice to see you again, Mrs Harvey,' I said, rather too loudly as if deafness rather than memory loss was her problem. 'Thank your sister from me for the tea. I hope you feel better soon.'

She stared at me as if I had just walked in.

'Perhaps you could see me out, Mr Harvey.'

He followed me to the front door. I looked around. No sign of Molly. That was good. When he had returned I had longed for her to join us. Now I knew this had to be just between him and me. He stood in the doorway. I turned back towards him.

'I know what you did.' I tried to sound as casual as if we were exchanging farewell pleasantries. 'You and Tom. He told me everything. You weren't there when he died. But he was. You supplied the means. One bottle of that horrible whisky and one bottle of her pills. The first easily replaced at any off-licence. The other a bit harder, but her sister sorted it out for you without ever suspecting what was going on. And after all that it's all been a waste. You thought getting rid of him would help her. And help you cope with her. And she's forgetting him anyway. It was all for nothing. Soon he could have been coming here every day, telling her all the details of his sex life, and she wouldn't know him from Adam. And as for the details, she'd have forgotten them in seconds. No time even to get shocked. Before you came in I was doing my best to restore some of her memories of him. So she could still feel a little guilt and pain. I have no idea if it worked or not. I don't suppose so. But you, you'll remember, won't you? And you'll remember that there is someone else who knows. Goodbye, Mr Harvey.'

I turned away swiftly, noticing that the fists were now clenching.

THIRTY-THREE

I ran towards the end of the street, realising almost immediately how out of condition I was, almost bumping into Molly who was waiting for me at the corner.

'How did it go? Are you all right?'

'No need to worry,' I gasped when I had at last caught my breath. 'She's all right and so am I. She never said a word. No idea if she understood anything of what I was saying but I said it anyway. Only problem was, we had a visitor. He came back early.'

Her hand flew to her mouth. 'Oh my God! I had no idea. It's almost unheard of for him to miss a night with his pals. That's why I arranged it for today.'

'He didn't miss. Just came home early. He had been to the pub. Maybe one of his mates didn't turn up and they decided to call it a night.'

'What happened?'

'I was stupid, I'm afraid. And reckless. But after talking to her and getting no response and seeing him standing there in front of me I was in no mood to stop. So I told him what I knew. Not in so many words. Not at first. We were polite, testing each other out. I was dropping hints and watching his reactions. I waited until I was on the doorstep before I told him directly. That was when he looked as if he might get violent. I decided it was high time I got the hell out of there.'

She stopped and turned to me.

'You're shaking, Alan.'

'I know. Can't seem to stop.'

'It's all right. You'll soon recover. And you did the right thing. Thank God you weren't hurt. Look, there are some things I want to tell you, about our family. I've been thinking about it for a long time, waiting for the right moment. Now it's come. It's not pleasant but I think you need to hear it.'

'All right. Go on.'

'Not here. We've a train to catch.'

It was an unassuming street of terraced houses about a mile from the northern docks. One end was dominated by a disused gasworks. At the other end the street was overlooked by a church spire, the plain white cross visible along the entire length. Smells of tar and fertiliser drifted in from the direction of the river.

'This was our house,' she said. 'The one at the end. Wonder who lives there now. I haven't been back since I was first married. I was hoping it would still be here. I expected it would. These houses were built to last. It hasn't changed. A new coat of paint on the door and window frames, that's all.'

The door gave straight onto the pavement. Dark red brickwork framed the tall windows, which had upper panes of stained glass in a flowery pattern. A secure, solid home, safe and welcoming, watching over the children playing hopscotch in the street immediately outside. A home that promised tea, warmth and bed when the day's play was done and hunger and fatigue beckoned. The scene would have changed little over the years. These children would be blessed with time and attention if not with material riches. I felt a pang of jealousy. I glanced at Molly. She was frowning, as if summoning up the courage to say what she had to say. Did these carefree children remind her of her own childhood? If so, there was no trace of nostalgia in her expression. And if her childhood had been content, why had she brought me there to tell me about it?

'Not a bad house, compared with the slums further up towards the city centre,' she said, at last. 'Perfectly respectable. And God keeping an eye on all of us from that bloody great church over there. St Teresa's. Our local. Full to bursting every Sunday. Yes, a nice three-bedroom house.'

She stopped. I waited. She turned towards the house before continuing, as if summoning the ghosts of her memories from deep within its walls. She spoke very quietly. I stepped up beside her so I could hear her.

'Three bedrooms. But there were seven of us. Four boys and three girls. The boys came first. One after the other. Then, after a gap, us girls. One after the other. The boys all left as soon as they were old enough. Went off to far-flung parts of the globe. Canada, New Zealand, Australia. Never heard from them since. No idea if they're dead or alive. Anyway, when we were all together in that house we had to share. Naturally. Clothes were hand-me-downs. One bicycle with bent wheels and rusty chains, passed among the boys, depending on who had a paper round to do. The last one to have it had to fix it for the next one. We girls shared as well. Hair combs, ribbons, bits of make-up when we were a bit older. Oh, we weren't poor. Only nobody had all the stuff you have these days. No, we were comfortable, respectable. Father had a good job down at the docks. He was on the staff, not the piecework labour force. Had a regular salary. Wore a suit and tie to work. Homburg hat. That was his pride and joy. He looked after it like it was a family pet. None of us kids was allowed to go near it. Mother didn't go out to work. Had her hands full at home. But we got by.'

She turned to me. There were tears in her eyes.

'That was when it started. When we were a bit older, I mean. I look at these children here and I wonder, is time their friend or their enemy. What does life have in store for them? Do they even think about it? I'm sure they don't. That's what makes childhood so wonderful, don't you think, when you have enough, enough of food, of shelter, of love? Just enough, that's all you need. Then you don't think of time or the future. You just live from moment to moment, trusting it will be all right. Why shouldn't it be? It's been all right up to now, so why shouldn't that go on? That's what we thought, if we thought about it at all. But all the time the future was marching towards us and we never saw it coming. Yes, we were older by then. I'm not talking sixteen or seventeen. Not yet. I'm talking about a time before that. You see, we had already grown up very suddenly, some years before you're supposed to. I was eleven. Catherine was nine. The boys had already gone to seek their fortunes.

'Up to then, Father had rather taken us girls for granted. He was like most men in those days, I suppose, never one to show any feelings. He was distant and formal. When he came home from work we were not to disturb him until he had had his tea and read the evening paper. After that we could sit in the same room with him and read, even chat a bit among ourselves, so long as we were not too noisy. But he did not seem to mind us. Sometimes he would ask about how our day at school had gone. When it was bedtime we could kiss him on the cheek and say goodnight.

'Now all that started to change. He was taking a new interest in us. He had a choice to make, you see. One of us, to do a special job for him.'

Her voice broke. I put my hand on her shoulder.

'Molly, you don't need to do this.'

She shook her head. 'Yes, I do, Alan. You know I do. That's why we're here. I can't go back now. You must promise to listen and not say anything.'

'I promise.'

'The job, the special job, was at night, in bed, between him and our mother. So there could be no more of us. She'd started having us at seventeen. There had been more. After Catherine. Twins, a girl and a boy, then another boy. All died within a year of birth. They were weak, underweight. There were all sorts of infant illnesses around in those days. Then she had a miscarriage. Future pregnancies were too risky. Even if they had another child and it survived, they couldn't have afforded it. The future had arrived in other ways, too. He'd lost his job. It was the start of the Great Depression. I remember the night he sat us down, the three of us, next to each other on the bench in the kitchen where we had our meals. It was like we were at school. Only school was safe. Home was not. Not any more. He went along the row of us, touching our cheeks, telling us how pretty we had grown. We could tell he was choosing one of us, though of course we had no idea what for. It could so easily have been me. I thought for a moment it was. But then he moved on to her, let his hand linger on her cheek, gave her a special smile, whispered something into her ear I could not hear. That night, she moved into their bed. She and I had been sharing a bed until then. She never said anything to me. She got undressed, put her nightdress on, all as usual, then left the room and did not come back in. That became her new routine. The next morning I found out where she had gone to spend the night. We shared household chores and it was my job to make the beds. Catherine had this old teddy bear. Had had it for years. An eye missing and one arm half torn off but she still loved it. So did I. It was always in bed with us, lying between us. Now I was on my own at night. She had taken the teddy with her. Into her parents' marriage bed. It was there in the middle when I made their bed, in the space where her little body had lain, between the two of them. She took it there to make her feel less lonely, I suppose, less afraid. Alan, for God's sake, it could have been me.'

She put her face in her hands, her shoulders shaking.

'But it wasn't you, was it? He chose your younger sister. He chose Catherine. When she was only nine.'

So that was her curse, bestowed in the form of a blessing. The curse of the chosen.

'Let's move on, Alan. I can't bear to be here any longer. There's a park on the other side of the church. Let's go there.'

When we reached the park she took my arm.

'They were close all the time after that. He ignored my other sister and me. He talked to her all the time, played with her. I heard the things he promised her. That her life would be a fairy tale. That she would have everything she wanted. He was making it up to her with his promises of castles in the air and Princes Charming coming to woo her. Making it up to her for what he was doing to her at night. She took it all in. She doted on him. Only you can't make up for bad deeds with good words, can you?'

'And your mother knew all about it and condoned it.'

'Of course. It was an arrangement they had agreed between them. It was a relief for her. No more unwanted attention. No more danger of unwanted pregnancy. This is why in recent years I have tried to forgive Catherine, hard though that is. Because it could so easily have been me.'

'She chose her husband because he would never see her that way, never remind her of those times with her father. He would never look at her with love, but at least he would never look at her with lust. And she thought that was a price worth paying.'

'Yes. That was the worst of what Father did to her. Made it impossible for her to have a normal life. At the same time he made her feel special and entitled. Real life came along with all its disappointments and she had never learned how to cope. It was not the life he had promised her. Where were the fairy tales now, and the Princes Charming? She could not ask him. He had long since passed away. It's funny, but at the time when it all started I hated her. I was intensely jealous because she had all Father's attention.'

We left the park and walked up to the front of the church. I knew there was more, that what she still had to tell me had something to do with that grotesque temple of guilt which had loomed over their street and their lives. How terrifying that massive House of God must have seemed to them when they were just small children, how impossible to escape its accusing shadow. Would she want us to go inside? She shook her head as if she had heard my unspoken question. From within, an unseen, all-seeing presence had watched over their early lives, all their deeds and thoughts. Fear and pain dwelt within, not love or forgiveness. It was some minutes before she could continue.

'We came here every Sunday, of course, dressed up to the nines, even when we no longer had any money. Confession on Saturday evening so as to be pure for Communion on Sunday. After she married she carried on going to church. But it didn't feel right for her. She was desperate for the Absolution you get from the sacrament of Confession, but you only get that if you confess all your sins to the priest. There was one sin she could not confess. I don't know this for a fact, of course. She never talked to me about what she told the priest. But I'm sure she never told him about that. You know what I'm referring to. Because from the time when it started she stopped going to Communion. I asked her why. She still went to Confession so surely she had to be in a state of grace. She said it was because she had not confessed it all. So she wasn't in a state of grace. So it would be a sacrilege to take Communion, to take the Body and Blood of Christ into her. I understood later what she meant. You see, she didn't see it as something done to her. She had to do certain things to him, perform certain acts. Because those were her actions she saw them as sins. Her sins. But there was no way she could go to the priest and tell him. Even if she could have found the words he wouldn't have believed her. He would have told her she had seduced her father and was blaming her father for her own wickedness. He would have called her a child of the devil. She would never have been absolved.

'So there she was, married and a mother, still going to church, still afraid to confess the sin, as she saw it, which had blighted her whole life. Then when Simon came along, she persuaded him to take on the burden. He substituted for her. She stopped going to church when he became an altar boy. He was atoning for her sin, her original sin, while knowing nothing at all about it. And when he stopped, she was exposed again, unabsolved before God, unable to confess.'

'And trapped in a loveless marriage, one of her own choosing.'

'She was always lonely. When Father chose her, she could no longer be close to her mother or her sisters. She could not make friends. She was too special, too different. Maybe that was why she hoped Simon would be a girl. So that when her daughter grew up she could be the companion she had never been able to have. When she realised she would never have a daughter she became very depressed. I told you about the way she neglected Simon when he was a baby, pretended he was not there, hoped someone else would take him and care for him. Later she found uses for him. But it didn't work. Still burdened with her original sin, she was drawn into another sin, one which was not done to her, one in which she was not helpless, no longer a child. Simon is no longer in her life. Not just since his death. It had been that way for years, from the time he started to go his own way. When he went to college she removed all the memories of him around the house. You saw that. She threw away the photographs. Sold the piano. He came back for vacations and slept in his old room. But he was just a lodger. I never saw her speak to him. He seemed not to mind. He was probably relieved to be free of her attention.'

'Were you there when she got the news?'

'Reginald took the call from the Master. He already knew, of course. From Tom. Knew that they had succeeded, even if they had had to go further than the original plan of just scaring him. But they had to wait for the body to be found. Reginald must have put on a convincing show of surprise and shock when he took the call. I suppose he had been preparing himself for it. He decided not to tell her anything for the time being. He waited for Tom to come up. They asked me to be there when they told her. She didn't react. She said nothing. Just wore that hard expression which she'd been wearing for so long it had become part of her nature. Reginald told her he would have to go down to identify the body, but there was no real doubt that it was Simon. Again she showed no reaction. I stayed with her while Reginald was away. I remember him coming through the door. He just nodded to me. I tried to tell her again that Simon was dead, that he had drowned, that Reginald had just come back from identifying the body.

Nothing. I got her ready for the funeral, tried to explain yet again what it was about. If she did understand she never let on. I hoped she would at last start to grieve but that has never happened. Now it never will.'

EPILOGUE

I t is twenty years since the events I describe above. I have retired now, having saved enough from my bachelor existence to buy a small cottage in Devon. I cultivate my rose garden, grow vegetables and go for long walks. Through the college journal I keep in touch with the progress of some of my students. I have the satisfaction of knowing that a good few of them have found success in the different walks of life they have chosen. As you would have done, Simon. You would now be approaching your forties: tall, handsome, confident, secure in your identity, having lived to see the changes come about for which you longed.

Wherever you are now, you may know what has happened to the main characters in your drama. I will record their story nonetheless for any into whose hands this account may pass.

Before your mother was detained in secure accommodation for her own safety and for the continuous care she would soon need, she visited your grave of her own accord. She wandered away from home, as she had begun to do despite the watchful eyes of her husband and sister. On the first few such occasions she was found further along the street, sometimes escorted back by a helpful neighbour. This time she was not so easily located. The police were alerted. They took her description and promised to keep a lookout for her. After a few hours, Molly had an inspiration for which she could not account. She went to the church, said a prayer and then went round to the cemetery. She found your mother standing by your grave. Your mother had been there at the funeral but not since. Nobody had reminded her where it was. And if they had, she would not have retained the information. It was Molly who told me all this. We corresponded regularly. She would call in to see me on her occasional visits to Oxford.

What had happened? I have my theory, for what it is worth. Your mother's dementia did not work evenly on her memories. She had forgotten you, as she so desperately wanted and needed to. But as the disease progressed she forgot why she needed to forget. So you re-emerged from those depths where the memories of a son are seared so profoundly that they cannot be that easily erased. You called her to your graveside. Did she then recall your form, your face, your voice, even your name? No, all that had gone, in the absence of anything around her to keep those things before her fading mind. In its place was a palimpsest, formed of the indestructible impressions left within the soul of any mother by the mere fact that a child has passed through her body and out into the world. Do I still sound like an academic, expounding his pet theory of the creative processes of a centuries-dead author whose very name is not known for certain? If so, I cannot help it. That is what I am and what I do. I know you will understand and forgive.

Alban and I are still in touch. He is well known now as a historian and broadcaster. He has even written a book, on the Peterloo Massacre, wouldn't you know? He comes to visit me occasionally, with a delightful young man he describes as his partner. They are clearly very much in love. But there is an unspoken agreement between us not to talk of those times. I am sure his new love has no knowledge of them. I know you will be pleased for his sake that he has found happiness.

Major Max is also retired and has a cottage some miles from here. We meet from time to time for a drink and a chat, usually about gardening and the weather. Again we seem to be content never to refer to the events which brought us closer together than surely any don and head porter have been before or since.

Your parents both died within six months of each other. Your mother had already suffered a series of strokes while in the secure unit. She died quietly a few weeks later. Molly's health also declined, rapidly in the end. We never saw each other after my retirement. Last year a neighbour of hers wrote to tell me she had passed away, lung cancer finally claiming its due after years of heavy smoking. Molly had told her to let me know so I could attend her funeral. I did so gladly. It was an intimate, warm-hearted affair, where I realised how much she was loved by her friends and neighbours.

As for your father, his death, from a heart attack, followed soon on the event I have still to mention.

That same night, after we had left him in the barge, Tom, like you, slid silently into the embrace of the water, never to return. Nobody saw or heard anything. It was some weeks before his body was found and his identity established. He had not gone far. Nearby was a dark, fetid creek where discarded waste from the barges and overlooking houses had collected and into the midst of which he had drifted and become enmeshed. The papers told of the tragic end of a brilliant and promising young lawyer whose career he had himself ruined through fraud and alcohol abuse. The verdict was open, the coroner unable to determine whether he had deliberately taken his own life or fallen in by accident as a result of an excessive intake of alcohol. Nobody interviewed me about it. Sheila Black, schooled in discretion after all those years working for him, never told anybody she had given me directions to the barge.

How do I know it was that same night when it happened? Because of what Tom and I had both said, that it would end that night. I had only meant that we would pursue him no more. That was what Alban, Max and I had agreed, in the event that we heard a confession from his own lips. What Tom had meant by it only became clear when the news broke. Alban rushed round to see me as soon as he heard. Had I gone back to finish what we had started? There was an expression of horror on his face at the thought. He had only ever wanted justice, not revenge. Conventional justice could never be his. But justice of a sort had been there before him, in that wreckage of a man condemned by his own actions to an imminent death by whatever means. That was enough for him. I assured him that neither I nor Max had gone back. He nodded and placed his hands together. I know he was thinking of you in that moment. He then sat quietly in your chair for a few minutes while I made coffee and waited for him to regain his composure. At last he looked up and smiled, as if a great weight had finally been lifted from him. We have never talked about the matter since.

I arranged for your things to be sent on by van courier to me in college. When they arrived I asked Alban to come round and sort out anything he wanted to keep. He kept all your records and books. We donated your clothes to charity.

Then there was the little matter of the photographs. We had always assumed you had destroyed your copies, and so we had destroyed his, our way of putting the whole affair behind us. Now we knew you had kept yours and hidden them away. I suggested to him that things were different now. The photographs could no longer be used for pressure or blackmail. I explained why I thought you might have decided to keep them. Did he perhaps now feel the same way? I offered to hide them in my room in the same place I had hid his. When he decided he wanted them he only had to ask. If he preferred for them to be destroyed we would do it together. After his finals, just before he was due to leave Oxford to take up a scholarship in the States, he asked me to let him have the envelope. To the best of my knowledge he has it still.

I would like to say that the events of those two years changed my life, but that would be to overstate the matter, something against which I have constantly warned my students. My academic life continued as before. In one respect only was there a real change. I made a point of setting aside time once a term with each of my students over lunch or in a pub. I even tried to appreciate their favourite beers, though with limited success. All talk of work was forbidden at those times. I encouraged them to tell me about their lives before college, their friends, their families, their interests. One of them was musical, like you. I told him the story about Adrian Boult and Handel's *Largo*, the one my piano teacher had told me. I think he enjoyed it, as you might have done. Maybe they were baffled on those occasions but with the tolerance of the young they were happy to humour me. After all, a bachelor don is supposed to be a bit weird. So why disappoint them? Why not play the part to the full?

I gained a belated doctorate in my early fifties, though I never use the title. My few publications earned some respect in the very enclosed circle in which academics in my field move.

As time wore on and retirement loomed I became more and more of a curio, so different from the new generation of dons who followed me, all with stunning young wives and beautiful children, all skilled at building their reputations far beyond their specialisms through the media, all renewing the college with fresh sources of funding and dynamic research projects. Just at the time when I was beginning to realise I needed to move on and make way for someone in the new mould, a word was whispered in my ear that I might take on the mantle of Master for a brief period, Dr Groves having finally decided in his late seventies that it was time to give up the lodgings and move to his family home in the Cotswolds. Another father figure, someone from the passing generation, was called for to provide continuity and stability while a longer-term replacement was sought, someone who could cope with the bracing new financial climate. I got the message. They wanted me as a caretaker. I scotched the idea with indecent haste and probably unaccustomed rudeness and brought forward the date of my departure to the earliest possible moment. The new Master is a former captain of industry with no academic experience. Now money flows into the college coffers as never before.

And you continued, my dear Simon, to visit me in my room and sit in the chair where you first sat at your interview and later for your tutorials. I still do not feel I ever got to know you. Your life story was one of filling in the gaps in the lives of others, building up their hopes, coming to a tragic early end when you inadvertently threatened to destroy those hopes. Did I use you as well? Why was I so keen to admit you as a student? You would be the first to agree you were dazzling neither in your work nor your personality. But there was something else, something of much greater value. A gentleness, a patience, a premature seriousness, an understanding of life I would never achieve. You had no bitterness or self-pity. With what I know now I would have understood if you had. No, once you had discovered yourself, that crime for which your family could never forgive you, you dedicated your short life to beauty and truth, those two qualities which the poet Keats declared to be the same. Beauty of body and soul. Truth of love and humanity.

You lived and paid the price. I have not lived and there is a price to be paid for that. I pay it every day. I ache to have been what you were, to have known freedom and love, however briefly, to have seared into my memory until my last conscious moment the sense of touching and being touched. That ache is your gift to me and I accept it wholeheartedly. You breathed your last much too soon. But your young body had known what it was to worship and be worshipped. I have lived only in my mind, and in but a small part of it at that, the place where recording and logic and strict analytical judgement reside. What little you learned from me is petty and insignificant in comparison with what I learned from you.

There are some who will always believe that in loving the way you did you committed a sin, against divine decree or against society or both. I never believed that for one moment. Sin is what was done to you and Alban, an evil river flowing through many tributaries from its source, that original sin, that perversion disguised as love perpetrated by a father on a chosen daughter all those years ago in an ordinary family house in the shadow of a church.

I also understand my own sin. This is what you taught me above all else, that my choosing not to live has indeed been a truly grievous sin. *The wages of sin is death*, so St Paul tells us. Wages. What is earned and due to us. I do not fear death. It is my due. Nor do I await it with longing. Why should I? Death called for me long ago. I looked it in the eye, as we all must face what is our due. It took me by the hand and led me away. What remains, writing these words, this apparently living, breathing part of me that persists? What else but baggage that has been mislaid and will follow on a later plane.